The inaugural anthology
from artist collective
POC United

GRAFFITI

Edited by

Pallavi Dhawan
Devi S. Laskar
Tamika Thompson

aunt lute books
San Francisco

Aunt Lute Books
P.O. Box 410687   Print ISBN 978-1-879960-98-5
San Francisco, CA 94141   Ebook ISBN 978-1-939904-34-8
www.auntlute.com

Cover design: Poonam Whabi
Book design and typesetting: A.S. Ikeda
Senior Editor: Joan Pinkvoss
Artistic Director: Shay Brawn
Managing Editor: A.S. Ikeda
Production: Maya Sisneros, María Mínguez Arias, Kayla Rogers, Andrenne Harbin, and Cindy Ho

Publication of this book was made possible, in part, by support from the San Francisco Arts Commission, the National Endowment for the Arts, and the Sara and Two C-Dogs Foundation.

sfac

Library of Congress Cataloging-in-Publication Data

Names: Dhawan, Pallavi, editor. | Laskar, Devi S., editor. | Thompson, Tamika, editor.
Title: Graffiti / edited by Pallavi Dhawan, Devi S. Laskar, and Tamika Thompson.
Description: San Francisco, CA : Aunt Lute Books, [2019] | Summary: "Graffiti is the first installment in a themed, multi-genre anthology series called POC United. The aim of the POC United series is to foster literary spaces in which the work is drawn by forces other than the interests of the white imagination-interests that so often send writers of color down the path of centering oppression for exoticized consumption. In her introduction to the anthology, author and poet Elmaz Abinader says: "Graffiti hits like a playlist of street grinds, jigsaw puzzles, fairy tales and lyric dreams. ... Slashed on the wall of our literature, seeing it close in its moving colors and from afar in its searing declarations, Graffiti gives us just a taste of what writers of color do, unbound.""-- Provided by publisher.
Identifiers: LCCN 2019026261 (print) | LCCN 2019026262 (ebook) | ISBN 9781879960985 (paperback) | ISBN 9781939904348 (ebook)
Subjects: LCSH: American literature--Minority authors. | Racially mixed people--Literary collections. | Ethnic groups--United States--Literary collections.
Classification: LCC PS508.M54 G73 2019 (print) | LCC PS508.M54 (ebook) | DDC 810.8/0920693--dc23
LC record available at https://lccn.loc.gov/2019026261
LC ebook record available at https://lccn.loc.gov/2019026262

Printed in the U.S.A. on acid-free paper

10 9 8 7 6 5 4 3 2 1

CONTENTS

GRAFFITI

POC United

EDITORS' NOTE

What happens when whiteness is decentralized for writers of color? Where will the work take them when the focus is no longer the struggle, their oppression, or how their characters of color will be received by the white imagination?

To find out, we created POC United, an anthology series that serves as a literary safe space of creative play for writers of color far removed from the white gaze. A place where POC can focus on one another in solidarity. Where we can build together, with works that center neither "whiteness" nor "anti-whiteness." We joined forces with poet and novelist Devi S. Laskar to showcase original short stories, essays, and poems across all genres. Our inaugural themed collection is *Graffiti.*

We put out a call to writers whose work we admired and told them about what we were trying to do, that we wanted to acknowledge the ways in which writers of color already support one another by welcoming, centering, and cultivating that effort. We expected that the stories would come flooding in, with kick-ass characters and vibrant, graffiti-adorned settings. But, for some, the focus of this collection wasn't easy. Peel back the ongoing fight for civil and/or human rights, remove the need to describe a character using the "othering" language of white supremacy, get rid of the notion of creating a story that must be the "right fit" for a white publication with white editors catering to a white audience, strip the story of over-explainers and translations for the white reader, and some writers struggled with what to produce, as if the freedom to create a liberated and liberating work was confining.

We had to tell some writers to start again, remind them of how this collection would be different from all of the others. One wanted to write about a racist act that happened in Texas; another wanted to focus on police brutality. The 2016 presidential election was on the minds of many. But we wanted to create a space where the work is drawn by forces other than the interests of the white imagination that so often send writers of color down the path of centering oppression. All of that much-needed work is for a different anthology, we told them. Not this one. Not this time. We want the protagonist who can leap across rooftops without fear. We want a journey rooted in the hero's culture as if her heritage were the only one on the planet. We want a character who shouts, "Mashallah! Mashallah!" without italics, without footnotes, without an explainer in the text that follows. If the reader isn't following, she can look it up. If the reader isn't willing to do that work, this collection is probably not for her. We, both as editors and readers, wanted this anthology to appeal to a heterogeneous audience, so no one reader is likely to connect with all of the works via a path of shared cultural experience. With no explainers, readers are encouraged to connect in ways that don't run through the center of white consciousness.

And, after months of prodding, pushing, gentle reminders, and pulling, we—the editors and contributors—now have a collection that centers POC. We made it. WE made it. We MADE it.

Pallavi Dhawan and Tamika Thompson
Creators, POC United

Nayomi Munaweera

FOREWORD

I did my very first public reading at Litquake in San Francisco's Clarion Alley in 2006. Clarion Alley is a tiny lane in the Mission District, long famous for the spectacular murals and graffiti that adorn both sides of its entire length. There was something about the graffiti that spoke to me. Graffiti artists work in secret, in the dark, hiding from police. The public only sees the final product, not the process by which the piece was made, and this seemed quite analogous to the work of writing.

At the time I thought of myself as someone who wrote every day, who was working on a novel, mostly in secret, but I did not see myself as a writer. The definition of a writer, in my imagination, was still mostly white, still quite male. My parents' hard-working, first-generation, Sri Lankan–immigrant sensibility could not conceive of creative work as an enterprise worth pursuing and grappling with, especially at the cost of financial stability. Parental disapproval was seconded by the fact that I just didn't see people who looked like me writing. It was impossible to imagine being a writer because I didn't see *any* writers— or indeed, characters—that looked like me. I didn't imagine that the stories of people like me, stories of families like mine would interest an American audience that I imagined as monolithic and white.

Few writers become writers without first being readers. What first seeds the brain are the words of another writer, living or dead. It is this entangling, the loathing of, or falling in love with another writer's work that makes a person want to write. The project of literature is cumulative. A process akin to graffiti, the way an artist works a wall upon which others come to add and erase and add and erase until what remains is as far from the original as possible.

My first consciousness that brown people, black people were writing was stumbling upon Gabriel García Márquez's *One Hundred Years of Solitude* at the library in high school. That book was my gateway drug. I lived in its vivid dreamscape for weeks. I did not want to emerge, but when I did, I was voracious. In the next years I "discovered" Alice Walker, Toni Morrison, Toni Cade Bambara. Later Anita Desai, Salman Rushdie, Maxine Hong Kingston, Michael Ondaatje. But it wasn't until I found Shyam Selvadurai, a Sri Lankan writer, that I imagined, in some far part of my mind, being a writer. Finally I had seen myself reflected on the page, and the discovery was profound. I'm guessing that most, if not all, writers of color have had a similar trajectory. We did not grow up seeing ourselves on the page. It is an absence into which we had to write ourselves.

In these past years, writers of color have flourished, and our ranks have grown tremendously. Still, we work against a publishing industry that loves to pick "The One." This is the phenomenon in which an author from a certain community is picked to represent that community in totality, while all or at least most other voices from that community are ignored. We saw this elevation with Junot Díaz and Sherman Alexie, both of whom were touted as the voices of their people to the exclusion of any other Latino or Native voices at the very highest level.

For decades, The One in South Asian American fiction has been Jhumpa Lahiri. Although my writing is nothing like hers, I have been compared to her numerous times. I have even been called the "Sri Lankan Jhumpa." When I told a writer friend this, he burst out laughing and said, "Well. I'm called the gay Jhumpa, so there."

To be clear, I'm not complaining about being compared to Lahiri. It's a huge compliment, and I think she writes beautifully. So do Díaz and Alexie. But the problem with having The One is that the publishing world, mostly white, can pat itself on the back, saying that it has represented the Latino world, the Native world, the Black world, the South Asian world because it has showered literary blessings upon these chosen ones. White readers, too, can feel that they have paid attention to the literature of a certain community because they have read a book by The One. This is a kind of literary laziness. Now, of course, with both Díaz and Alexie reaping the consequences of past actions brought to light by the #MeToo Movement, there is a rush to find "the new Junot," "the next Alexie." I would argue that white writers do not have to face this gauntlet; there is a much wider field representing white experience.

The work of this anthology defies the idea of The One. It posits that none of us can express the immense and vibrant diversity of the communities we are supposed to represent alone (if that's even our desire). Instead, our work is cumulative, collective, informed by each other, in conversation and collaboration. In the vein of theme-based, multi-genre anthologies, the editors asked the authors to write pieces that would address the theme of graffiti. As the barrier to publication is higher for writers of color, the editors chose to emphasize works that have not previously been published, in this way amplifying the voices of the many writers celebrated in this collection.

The lush banquet gathered here is testimony to the brilliant work people of color are creating. In this book, you will find defiant short prose from Kirin Khan and 2018 PEN America Literary Awards—Los Angeles winner Vickie Vértiz, Sarah LaBrie's fabulous nonfiction essay about the difficulty of writing itself, illuminated poetry from American Book Award winner Tongo Eisen-Martin as well as from three-time Pushcart Prize nominee Kay Ulanday Barrett, new fiction from award-winning fantasy author L. Penelope, and the work of so many other important writers. It has been a joy to read this book, and I congratulate everyone in it. I hope it finds its way into countless hands, especially those of young people of color looking to find themselves on the page.

Beyond the idea of The One, beyond the concerns of the white publishing industry and the white readership, writers of color need to investigate how we relate to each other. How do we as people of color start to understand our divergent and yet so very similar experiences? How do we build alliances across vast diversity? How do we, as it were, write the graffiti that sinks our mark onto the page of this world together?

In this, graffiti is an apt metaphor. Graffiti is collaborative and cumulative. It wrestles for life, it is illegal, it is rebellious, it is renegade, it does not listen to authority about where and when and how it will be. It claims space. As writers of color, these are lessons to take deeply to heart. We need to read each other's work. We need to come to know each other's stories as well or possibly better than we know the dead great whites. We need to teach each other's books, give each other (paid) gigs, recommend each other to book clubs, write each other blurbs and reviews. This is how we support and elevate each other. In this way, we replace the idea of The One with multiplicity.

Recently, I found myself back at Clarion Alley. I walked along the narrow street and marveled at the graffiti. A few of the murals were unchanged, but most had been drastically altered over time. A favorite of mine, a simple heart with the words, "we're all in this together" had been repainted in thick layers until it was bulging off the wall, a living, beating organ. It spoke to the layering that happens over time, one artist building upon the work of another until what we have is a thick crust of meaning, a bricolage, a collective in collaboration.

I would remind us all, gathered in this anthology, that we are indeed "all in this together." The work of any of us amplified is a boon to all of us. What unites us is the insistent need to story-tell, to insist that we too belong and that we will mingle our stories, we *will* write large our truths upon the face of this world.

Elmaz Abinader

YOUR SPOT ON THE WALL

Introduction

Where are your words welcome? Where do you have permission to scribble, scrawl, romanticize, speculate, brag, retaliate, and narrate your own stories, visions, and ideas? Where can you find your space where you are not being examined, criticized, politicized, exoticized, or fetishized? For writers of color, those spaces are few and far between. Marginalized in the mainstream, outnumbered in the classroom, we are constantly confronted with pervasive feelings of censorship and exceptionalism.

In this collection, the editors, Pallavi Dhawan, Devi S. Laskar, and Tamika Thompson, invited writers from diverse genres to throw their writing on the wall, to jump over the fence with their verse and stories and flow without recrimination or consciousness of the white gaze. They were invited to play—to see the blank wall before them and follow inspiration and artistic impulse.

This freedom is welcome and important. The audacity of erasing the pending disapproval, responses, inquisitions dares to centralize the writers in *Graffiti* in their own canon. Without the defensiveness or even the meta-awareness of the character, the beat, the message, without all the hampering shit that comes, even from within the self, gone—well, the writer has wings. Toni Morrison said, "The point is not having the white critic sit on your shoulder and approve it."

Graffiti shows us ourselves, whoever we are: through the stories of family tensions, challenges, and love; through the examination of what writers do and how they do it. The works also expose lives that move in unexpected ways, how identity and society intersect, rendering characters who don't come from the cultural tropes we cling to—girls who live in mythologies, past and of their own creation, for instance, in Lin Y. Leong's iridescent story, "The Girl and the Moth." We find other girls who are surfing the complications of family, society, and love, and dare to redefine themselves in unexpected ways—like Faiza riding a skateboard in a sadar in Kirin Khan's story, "In Public."

Much happens in the streets in these stories: there is graffiti and there are characters who are as bold and present as words on the wall. From Suicide Jacq in Gary Dauphin's urban fantasy story to Maytra, who finds the lost and disenfranchised on the graffitied walls of Seattle, in Laura Lucas's "Nilscape." The stories represent lives that can't settle, that are filled with disruptions to the understanding of what's real.

The different notes that are sounded through these writings include tracking the plot process as in the meta-essay "On Writing" by Sarah LaBrie, or understanding one's role in "Stranded" by Pallavi Dhawan, or looking at the idea of addiction in "Loop" by L. Penelope. While these may sound like anyone's narratives—growth, understanding, identity—they permit the reader to see a world that includes people of color in familiar scenarios in contexts that don't jibe with template settings and triptych lives.

In "may we all refuse to die at the same time" by American Book Award winner Tongo Eisen-Martin, the poet says "I'm writing poems for the rest of my life again," emphasizing that the threat of artistic extinction, of human death, leads to a reckoning with forces. One of the forces pounding in the pavement of this book is "yes." Rendering the body or autopsying language, both Devi S. Laskar in "grə-fē'tē" *and* Alycia Pirmohamed in "Letter to My Body" find the need for the positive in the dark—whether that is found in the streets or on the body.

Graffiti hits like a playlist of street grinds, jigsaw puzzles, fairy tales, and lyric dreams. The dimensions, the angles, the many perspectives, the linguistic complexity and blessed boldness let us know that these writers of color felt their privilege as artists. If only for this one project. Slashed on the wall of our literature, seeing it close in its moving colors and from afar in its searing declarations, *Graffiti* gives us just a taste of what writers of color do, unbound.

Elmaz Abinader

Devi S. Laskar

GR∂-FĒ'TĒ

If I were Italian, all this would be in plural.

Me, myself, and I forming a "we." Sort of like a royal "we," a "we" that remains unamused.

In Italian, graffiti is plural, it cannot be singular.

As if the black "I" were not enough to stand on its own on this white page of a world.

As if the black "I" were blind to the possibility of beauty the illustrated walls could provide.

But I'm not Italian.

I'm American.

And, here, graffiti is singular.

All it takes is one.

Here, in America. Still breathing American air, still looking out the window at drought-stricken American trees, browning American grass.

On the maps, it says I'm close to the Pacific, and yet I can neither smell the salt air nor hear the waves lap the shore like a thirsty dog.

Everywhere I go, your Rubicon has already been marked, evidence that you arrived, you analyzed, and you conquered with spray cans and bubbled letters, with the faces you conjured, some with pointed stares emanating from the sunken eyes, some with aviator shades covering the windows to the wild souls.

Sometimes, I try to find meaning, clues in the densely gathered shapes you've left behind. Sometimes I can make out the Vitruvian man spread-eagle against the wall.

Is that you?

Sometimes the "I" is an affirmation.

Yes, I am alive. Yes, there are ten trillion stars in the sky, and I will neither see them all nor name them all before I die.

But while I'm here, still breathing this American air, still painting my pictures, and looking for you in every illustrated street corner, I will try.

Monique Quintana

BiRTHDAY SPELLS

On her thirtieth birthday, Maggie Gonzalez lost her smile. This isn't hyperbole. She literally couldn't smile. She had just gotten out of biology class at the JC, and was having her birthday dinner with her boyfriend, Jesse, and their daughter, Espy, at a Mexican restaurant that used to be another kind of restaurant in the eighties. The whole place was lined with bamboo shoots, and the bar had a string of white lights and a thatched roof. It kind of looked like something you would see on a postcard from a gift shop, but it was still charming, and it was still Maggie's favorite place to drink on-the-rocks margaritas. It took a while for her to figure out that she couldn't smile.

Since she was born, she had been called stoic as a statue. In all her little-girl pictures, the ones with her curly black hair, she usually looked sad, or sometimes even mad, but at least sometimes she would smile, like when someone said something funny or she saw a boy that she really and truly liked. But when she got her birthday tequila shot at the restaurant, she knew something was up. Her daughter was smiling at her, and Jesse was too, but she could not reciprocate. There was only a little bit of joy left in her and nothing to show for it.

She knew what Jesse was thinking, that she was ungrateful, that she wasn't happy with the gifts they'd bought her, wrapped carefully in bags, or for the teddy bear stuffed balloon they had dipped glitter-pink. That's what happens when you get a girl from the north side of Shaw, he said. That's what you get. Never happy. No smiles.

How was school? Jesse asked, as he stirred his lime margarita.

Since when did you start drinking those, babe?

I told him those drinks were for girls, Mom.

Espy stuck a finger in her father's dimple while he sipped the drink.

How was school?

Good. Good.

I was talking to your mom.

It was ok. We dissected little hearts. Fetal pig hearts.

Ewwwwww. That's fucking gross.

But the little pigs looked really peaceful, like they were sleeping. Once you have their chests cut open, it doesn't feel so bad.

That was when the waitress walked over with the tequila shot, and a big straw sombrero that she plopped on Maggie's head sideways.

Let's get a picture of this, Mom. You look so funny.

Espy grabbed her father's phone to take a picture.

Maggie felt her face grow hot, and she looked around because the entire restaurant was packed. Everything was in its place—the colored bottles at the bar, the middle-aged white women with their frothy daiquiris in the corner, the speckled fish swimming in the tank on the wall, the low and beautiful hum of the mariachi music, Jesse and Espy looking at her, laughing like cartoons, Espy with her curly black hair and Jesse with his buzzed head—they were all there in their place, but Maggie could not smile; her mouth would not let her, like she was wearing a cheap Halloween mask made of rubber and her skin was not her own. No smile.

Ok, Mom, if that's what you want for your birthday picture. You look pissed or something.

The waitress came back to the table with a vanilla cream cake dotted with dark chocolate shavings, and "Maggie" scrawled in cursive cherry.

Dad, why does the cake look busted?

I know. The people at the store told me the cake decorator was sick, and they had to have one of the clerks do it. Sorry. You're just going to eat it anyway.

I like my birthday cake. I'm glad we're here. I didn't think we were going to do anything today. You always say birthdays are just another day.

I would have complained about the cake more, but my friend's the manager right now, and I didn't want to look like a dick.

That was nice of you, Dad. I wish you felt like that all the time.

Espy pulled a small box out of her purse and handed it to Maggie.

It's something little. From me and Dad. I hope you like them.

It took a while for Maggie to open up the tiny gold box because Espy had wrapped it tight in strips of black and red lace ribbon. Inside the box was tissue paper folded and taped in a square, and inside the square was a pair of silver skull earrings with rhinestones that studded its head and eyeball sockets. They were just what Maggie wanted. She had never seen skulls that shape before. Every part of that skull's face—the forehead, the jaw, and the nose—seemed in balance. Every part of the face seemed beautiful.

I love these. Where did you get them?

We got them online. I found them and Dad paid. It's ok if you don't like them.

No, I love them.

Maggie took off the earrings she was wearing and put on the skulls. She lifted her hair so they could see.

See, I love them.

When Jesse got up to pay the bill, Maggie noticed that Espy had a small spiral notepad on the table, and was sketching something in it. She had been doing that since she was a toddler. Maggie would find little notes and drawings all over their apartment. Maggie would pick them up, and put them in a drawer for safekeeping, but now that Espy was in the sixth grade, she always kept them nice and neat in a notebook.

Espy made a face at Maggie.

What?

What? I can't look at you? You're my daughter.

It just makes me feel weird, that's all.

Espy scooped up her notebook, and her leftover enchilada box, and made her way out of the restaurant.

When they got back to their apartment, their neighbor Crystal was sitting on her balcony smoking and staring at the moon. She was wearing pink pajama pants and a tank top.

Hey, birthday girl. How does it feel to be thirty?

It feels like just another day to me.

Crystal looked at Jesse, rolled her eyes, and laughed.

This girl kills me. She really does. Have a good night guys. I mean y'all. I've been trying not to say you guys. It's the hardest habit to break in my life.

Crystal, is it cool if I ride with you to work tomorrow? Do you still have Doctor's car?

Yep, we don't have to go too early. Dr. Ramos wants me to go pick up some shit at the lab.

'K, knock loud though.

You know it.

Espy dropped the gifts on the living room floor and let the balloon float up to the low popcorn ceiling of the cold apartment. Maggie flipped a switch, and the heater came alive with a boom, which made Jesse groan softly because he liked it better when it was cold. He got hot easy. Espy went to her room and closed her door almost all the way, which Maggie found to be strange because she usually left it open, especially when the tree branches were tapping on the windows like they were doing then. Maggie wondered if it would rain; she was actually hoping that it would, since the rain always made her feel kind of happy, and she could use something to make her feel that way then. Jesse had already scampered off to the bathroom inside their bedroom, and she could hear the shower running, and faintly feel the warm mist that was coming out the door. He likes it cold, but he takes boiling hot showers. That doesn't make sense, she thought to herself.

She took off the scrub top and pants she had worn to work, to class, and to dinner, and threw them like a pink puke pile on the floor.

She rolled over on her stomach and pulled her cigarettes out of her favorite drawer. She lit one and flipped through a glossy new magazine that she had taken from the waiting room at work. She contemplated getting her hair dyed blonde—not butter blonde, but sort of a pale, straw-man blonde that might do better to compliment her skin tone, which Jesse told her was like caramel or mocha latte, something he told her because he was bad at giving compliments. Yeah, she thought, I would look great with blonde hair. Other women with dark skin had blonde hair, so why the fuck not? She was thirty after all, and it was time she grew up and looked more like a woman. Maybe she would scrounge up some money and buy a bottle of Chanel No. 5 or Youth-Dew. No, she thought, remembering how her grandma dotted her bra with the same stuff even days before she died. Maybe those perfumes in ten years or twenty, but not now, not yet.

She climbed under the sheets and sniffed them because she had just washed them that morning when it was still dark outside. She realized that maybe smoking a cigarette in the lily-fresh linen might not be the best thing, and she put the cigarette out on her nightstand. Little bits of ash snuffed out of the tray and made her sad. She could hear her Youth-Dew grandma call her cochina, the rasp of her voice ringing through her head and making her shiver. She imagined her grandma shaking her head at the dirty dishes in the sink and whacking the dust off the ceiling fan with a broom. No one would ever think to buy that woman a balloon with a teddy bear inside. She would have popped the motherfucker and thrown the bear in the Goodwill give-away box.

Jesse came out of the bathroom and sniffed the air.

Were you smoking in here?

Yeah.

I told you not to do that shit.

He put on his boxer briefs, slapped the elastic, and pulled his pipe out of his favorite drawer and lit it, and his piss-smelling bud speckled the bedroom.

This smells better than that, he said, touching Maggie's mouth with his fingertips. His fingers felt spiderlike, and he smelled like a deep green forest, and when he kissed her hard on the mouth, he still tasted like the girly lime margarita he had at the restaurant, and when he turned her on her stomach, Maggie noticed that the door was still open a sliver, and she thought she saw Espy peeking inside, so she jumped up, and looked down the hallway for her little girl. All she saw was the warm glow under Espy's bedroom door, looking like a UFO light, and she could hear Espy playing the nighttime dedications on her brand new boom box. Maggie got back in bed, and Jesse got behind her and rocked slowly until he came, and then he played spiders in between her legs, one last birthday gift, until she came, and he rolled over and fell into his tequila sleep.

Maggie put on her pajama pants and hoodie and went outside to the balcony to smoke another cigarette. Crystal was still outside, painting her toenails black and yelling at someone on the phone, her voice scratchy with a cough that she just couldn't get over. Maggie sucked on the cigarette and tried to figure out who Crystal was talking to. Soon, a helicopter began to circle in the sky, its lights flashing on the complex and the high school across the way.

They're looking for somebody. That motherfucker must be on foot, Crystal said, getting up on her tiptoes because her nails were only halfway done.

Someone in one of the apartments opened their bedroom window and yelled at Crystal to shut her fat fucking mouth, and she told them to come outside and make her. It wasn't even midnight yet. When Crystal got back on the phone, Maggie realized that she was talking to her older brother, Seth. Maggie had a sort of thing for Seth—not a full-blown crush, but something just hanging in the air, like the helicopter making hula-hoops in the sky. Her cigarette was now a nub, and so she flicked it into the shrubs below, watching the little meteor flicker down in the dark. Maggie's and Crystal's balconies were connected like two kidneys, except one of the light bulbs on Maggie's patio had blown out, so she was sitting half in the dark. Crystal was in full glow, like she was on stage, and even though she was in her pajama pants, she still had on a full face of makeup, with brown lipstick and her liner winged out in tiny triangles that made her large eyes look even more beautiful.

What are you doing out here, princess?

I hate when you call me that. Don't call me that. It drives me crazy. Princess princess princess.

That's the second helicopter that's flown over here this week.

I wonder if they can see us? Crystal said as she leaned over her balcony, pulled up her tank top, and flashed her breasts to the helicopter sky.

No, I think that was for nothing.

What did you guys do today?

Went to eat.

Did you get a buzz?

No. Jesse did though.

Thirty's a big one. So, how do you feel?

I feel nothing. I could care less.

If you're saying that you could care less, that means you still care. You want me to eat you out for your birthday?

Maggie looked at her and said, No that's ok, and she wanted to laugh.

Girl, I was just kidding. I know you like dick and only dick. Crystal got up and left Maggie in the cold and the dark. She shut the sliding glass door like a guillotine, and yelled, See you in the morning, from the other side.

Maggie watched the helicopter teeter off into the ether and sat on the old leather couch with her legs crisscrossed like a pretzel. She heard the vrooming sound of one of the laundry-room washing machines go on, a sound to match the swaying of the trees, and the sky still didn't rain, even though she wanted it to. She could see that Espy's light was still on in her bedroom window, and Maggie felt worried, but she knew that Espy would wake up even before the sun came up without complaint, and it was no use scolding her now.

The bear balloon had gotten caught in the kitchen-ceiling fan, so Maggie untangled it, and let it bounce around the kitchen, a bit like a brown baby in a uterus. She noticed just how pretty it was. It was a girl bear with long black eye lashes and a pink and red polka dotted bow, and she had a little card around her neck that said, To M, and Maggie wondered if that meant to Maggie or to Mom. She didn't really know. She wrapped the balloon string around her wrist like it was a tourniquet and went to tell Espy goodnight.

Espy had fallen asleep with the lamplight on, like she always did. She fell asleep with her clothes on too, so Maggie undressed her half-way, so she could be comfortable, and Espy only fluttered her eyelids a bit, and mumbled something about birthday cake. Just as she was about to hit the light switch, Maggie saw Espy's notebook opened to a dog-eared page, and, looking closer, she saw something that looked like her own face. It wasn't the little-girl drawings that she was used to, with the big doll eyes and mouths. It was definitely Maggie's paper twin. The curly dark hair, and slanted eyes, and the elf ears that had been the bane of her life. She looked closer and saw that in her ears were her brand-new birthday earrings, studded with pink ink and pencil-lead dots, but what got to Maggie the most was the mouth, her lips, full and red and sewn in stitches, in beetle-black ink that wouldn't go away.

THE FACE READER

It was my third session with Peggy, the Freudian/Jungian psychoanalyst with a prescription pad, who charged two hundred seventy-five dollars an hour for chitchat. Sitting in her cold, minimalist, all steel-and-glass office on a stark, Bauhausian, black leather couch stripped of all edges and meaning made me shrivel, so I took a deep, relaxing breath and spread my arms along the length of the couch to compensate. Peggy returned from the kitchenette and handed me a steaming cup of coffee. Its warmth was oddly comforting. She sat across from me in a rectangular leather armchair with a polite, plastered smile. I let my breath out.

Last session, Peggy had asked me to write down five rules, spoken or unspoken, obeyed by me as a child at home.

"Let's start," she said while I fidgeted around my pants pockets, looking for the list I had scribbled on a torn sheet on the cab ride over.

Peggy was in her fifties with brown hair, grey, dispassionate eyes, and the voice of a strict, Catholic pre-school teacher. She wore a black suit with a brown-striped top underneath and a golden bracelet with a tiny oval watch. I cleared my throat.

"#5: Do well in school."

"Was it spoken or unspoken?"

"It was not unspoken," I replied after some thought.

"Next?" she continued.

POC United

"#4: Eat everything on your plate."

Peggy just nodded. She now seemed as bored by this exercise as I was. I should have prepared better, I thought. I am wasting money by not taking this seriously.

"Your mother enforced it, right?" she asked.

"Yes, she did."

"Where is your mother now? Do you speak to her often?"

"She lives in a small town in South India. Yes, I do still speak to her, but not often."

"Why not?"

"I don't know. I couldn't stand the way she looked at me, as if this were my fault; her pitying, helpless, dog-eyed look."

"Why do you think that? Why was she afraid for you, I mean."

"I don't know. It was worse than the taunts of the colony kids."

"So you left home after high school," she said.

"Yes, I did."

She went back to scribbling in her notebook.

"#3: Avoid bad company." This was turning out be a snoozefest. I could spice it up, I thought, and told Peggy about how my father discouraged my friendship with Sapan because he visited video game parlours that were fronts for gambling dens.

"He was right as usual; Father always was. Sapan flunked tenth grade twice and, soon after, we drifted apart."

"Your dad mellowed since, you said last time. Where is he now?"

"He is dead," I snapped. Didn't she know this already?

"I am sorry," she said, lifting her arms. She sat further back in her chair.

"No, no, no, I am sorry." My apology came out as soon as I saw her recoil. "I am just angry, remembering how I wasn't even allowed to attend his funeral. My visa had expired, and I couldn't leave the country; if I did, I couldn't have come back."

I broke the awkward silence with, "#2: Be disciplined."

"What do you mean—oh! Was your father very strict?" she said.

"Yes, like a drill officer."

Peggy just nodded, and a face floated before my eyes. Large swaths of silver hair shining under an airplane's reading lamp—the Face Reader! It took Peggy three sessions for $925, and the Face Reader three minutes and 0 rupees, to get to the same place.

It was the summer of 1993—I was in eleventh grade. I remember Father coming home one day with a surprise: three plane tickets to Madras to visit Grandma. His business was taking off, and we could afford plane tickets now, he said, when Amma scolded him for spending so much. It made Amma smile for the first time in months. No more twenty-four-hour train rides in the Madras Mail in the heart of summer. But I loved the Madras Mail. I liked staring for hours at the barren rice farms, at the dry riverbeds and the brown trees coated with dust, at the telephone poles with lines of black crows. I would see the skin of the earth broken under the harsh scrutiny of the sun, the mighty Godavari River that had shriveled into a stream. But not even the sun, hotter than the devil's cauldron, could stop the peddlers at the railway stations—the chai-wallahs, the bhel-wallahs, the juice-wallahs—who would besiege the passengers. Each station had a different specialty, a different treat for me—masala chai in earthen cups, icy watermelon juice, and my favorite: sugarcane juice with lots of ice and a hint of lime. As the train progressed into the heart of South India, the treats would change. Now they became brown vadas with red and green chutney, coconut water, curd-rice with red pickle, pedas, and all of it downed with cold buttermilk spiced with green chile and cumin. The treats shortened the train journey, and our full stomachs put us to sleep.

All of that was replaced by the Bombay airport—a giant white building with pockmarked ceilings and gleaming floors awash in white fluorescent lights. In the Madras Mail, local villagers—fare-dodgers—would hijack our seats with impunity, but the airport was full of policemen with rifles. I remember the air hostess, perhaps sensing my anxiety, flashed me a pearly perfect smile. The brass name tag pinned to her orange blouse said Ranjeeta Nair.

Amma sat across the aisle, flipping through the inflight magazine, *Shubh Yatra*.

I glanced at my co-passenger in the middle seat, and we exchanged hellos. She was a kindly, middle-aged woman with bright, piercing eyes.

"You know, I can read faces," she said to me halfway through the flight after some small talk. "Can I try?"

"Sure? Is that like palmistry?" I remembered Saurabh claiming he could read palms. I didn't believe him. I thought it was an excuse for him to hold a girl's hand. All Saurabh said after looking at my palm was that I would have a long life and become rich. They all say that. Astrologers. Palmists. Numerologists. Mother has seen them all.

"Your father is very strict, isn't he?"

"He isn't strict anymore," I retorted, turning away from her, as if hiding my stripped self.

"I am sorry, I am sorry," she mumbled a few words of apology, while I wondered what else was etched on my face. Like Amma, I buried myself in the *Shubh Yatra* magazine, and the Face Reader closed her eyes and went to sleep like nothing happened.

I asked Peggy, "Do you think someone's past can be reflected on their face?"

She was silent for almost a minute, while I began daydreaming about life back home, before the money, before the planes.

"Hmmm. I don't think so," she finally said. "Perhaps in cases of serious trauma. But even then I doubt it—okay, so, what's number one?"

"#1: Never hit Vishu. Unspoken."

"Oh! Interesting. Why? Did you bully Vishu a lot?"

"No."

"Then why was it a rule?"

"You see, when we were young, Vishu was devoted to me. Vishu followed me everywhere and did anything I asked. This made my parents worry that I would take advantage of him."

"Did you?"

"No, wait, yes, a little; but nothing out of the ordinary."

"Ok, can you elaborate further on what exactly you understood this unspoken rule to be?" I caught her gaze flickering at my gimpy leg.

"It was understood, time and again, that if I ever hit him, I would suffer twice as much. And I did."

"Did you often suffer the consequences of violating that rule?"

So now we finally came back to my parents. I was dreading this not-your-fault-your-parents-fucked-you-up psychobabble.

"Well, not often," I replied, "but sometimes, but what he did was normal. Parents hit you; it's not a big deal. I was hit in school as well."

"You know," her voice indignant, "the trauma is the same, whether you are Indian or American."

No it's not, I thought. We are not the same. I was sick of being fit into their little boxes. How many Indians, Chinese, or Africans did Freud treat before he came up with his ego, superego, Oedipus crap?

"Tell me about a time that he hit you," she continued.

"Any time?"

"Yes."

"Okay, I just want to say, most kids in my colony got beaten by their parents much more than I ever did."

"Just tell me one incident."

"Well, there was this time he beat me with Mom's powder puff."

"A powder puff?"

"Yes, but this one was pink with a long plastic handle, it was used for applying talcum powder on your back. We found one in her room that evening, and started hitting each other with it. With the puffy side, I mean."

Peggy still looked confused.

"We then powder-puffed the walls of the bedroom, making fuzzy, six-inch, white circles all over. The harder we hit, the more distinct the circles got.

"I then convinced Vishu to take off his shirt, so I could powder-puff him. I will make the perfect mark, I told him.

"I saw Vishu's naked back. It was soft and unblemished—like him. As I swung, something perverse, an anger—a tamasic impulse—took over, and I hit him harder than I should have, trying to make the perfect circle of powder."

"With the powder puff?"

"Yes, of course with the puffy side hitting his back; the branding came out perfectly on his back, a distinct circle of white talcum powder on his dark skin. I smiled at my success, but then Vishu started wailing—ooooooooooOOOOOO. Sshhh shhhh, I said, afraid that Father, in the other room, would hear. It only made him cry louder. He was mad at me, he wanted me punished. Our parents rushed into the bedroom. Father took one look at the scene, and his eyes turned red. He grabbed the powder puff from my hands and began beating me with it."

"With the puff?"

"No. With the plastic handle of the puff. I was on the bed, my hands and legs were up in the air, I kept saying: I am sorry, I am sorry. But the blows didn't stop."

"And then?"

"Then, what?" I said.

"What happened next?"

"Nothing. That must have been it. I don't remember anymore." My arms came out from somewhere. I looked at them like they were some strange appendages. I folded them neatly into my lap.

"No, tell me. This is important." Peggy's eyes drilled into mine.

Suddenly, a dam within my head breached. Images flooded my cranium.

Amma was trying to stop him. She couldn't; his rage was volcanic. Minutes passed, perhaps hours. The blows kept coming. Amma finally managed to grab his hand. "You will kill him!" she said; meanwhile, I leapt out of the bed and fled out of the house. Out of the gates, into the main road. Running as if he were pursuing me, pink powder puff in hand.

"I fled the house," I finally replied to Peggy.

"And?"

"And what?"

"What happened next?"

"Then it happened."

"It?"

"Oh, nothing," I said. "I don't remember, I was really young."

"How young?"

"Like thirteen."

"Then you must remember."

"I don't."

"You do. What happened next?"

The room felt colder. I could hear the rain start anew. I could hear it drum against the window, like Peggy's words drumming against my skull—prying it open.

"I hit a bus." My breath began to feel constricted.

"A bus!?"

"Or something, I don't remember—I ran into something, and woke up in a nursing home the next day."

"What happened?"

"I don't remember, like I said, I hit a bus or something."

"Why were you in a nursing home? Is that like a hospital?"

"Yes, it's a mini hospital run by a single doctor."

"Why were you in the hospital?"

"It wasn't a hospital, we call it a nursing home," I snapped.

"Fine, nursing home, what else do you remember? What happened?"

I was in her grip. Her gloved hands were tearing into my flesh, like a surgeon with a knife, probing, cutting open the flesh to get to that ulcer, that rotten tissue, that cancerous tumour, that boil needing extraction, irradiation, cauterization.

"I just remember my leg in a cast. That's all I remember."

"Your leg, which one?"

"Does it matter?" There was a glass wall inside of me trying to push her away,

My head began spinning.

"It was not his fault," I cried.

"I never said it was."

"You did, but it was not his fault, I was born like this. I am this." I pulled my pant leg up to display my banged-up ankle.

The rain had stopped. Peggy began scratching in her diary. The room seemed to echo her words: The patient hit a bus. The patient hit a bus.

"You mentioned meeting a Face Reader," she said, flipping back a few pages.

"I was careless, as usual. Never looking around, irresponsible, undisciplined. I ran into the bus. It was my fault."

"The Face Reader," she continued, as if she hadn't heard me. "Was that before or after this incident?"

"It wasn't a bus. I would be dead if it were one."

Peggy got up from her seat and walked to the kitchenette.

"I don't remember what it was that hit me," I said to her back as she grabbed a glass.

"Would you like some water?" she asked. The bitch. I hated her for sounding smug.

She poured herself a glass. I took the one she offered me.

"Do you feel better?" she asked after I gulped it down.

"I feel fine," I said. "There's nothing wrong with me. I feel fine."

Kirin Khan

IN PUBLIC

Faiza rode her skateboard down a small lane in her F-10 neighborhood, her sadar wrapped around her throat and over her head, safety-pinned in place so it wouldn't billow out to her sides. The black wool sadar was warm for March, but she liked how safe it made her feel, like she had a turtle shell she could retreat into, her own private space, no matter where she was. She didn't mind looking like a superhero, cape billowing, but she'd learned the hard way that, inevitably, the unpinned cloth would wrap around a wheel and fling her to the ground by the neck. Better to pin it.

People on the street, mostly men and boys, stared at her as she skated by, but no one said much aside from a young boy who shouted, "Mashallah! Mashallah!" as she passed, halal harassment that she shrugged off. Her kick scraped against uneven gravel and dirt. Push and glide—she rode out each push as long as she could, shifting her weight heel-toe to carve back and forth and stretch the ride out.

Since her family left the States a few months ago, she'd tried to adjust. Travel restrictions were getting tighter all the time, and the stuff she loved about American life was not worth the risk of never seeing her family again—she didn't fight her parents on it, just like she didn't fight them about most stuff when they got here. She understood that she shouldn't go places alone, that she'd have an easier time of things if she wore the sadar, and that some places required more covering and some places less, but she couldn't give up her longboard. It was a beauty, with grapefruit-sized, neon-lime wheels that made the uneven street rideable, and clear grip tape so the blond wood grain showed through the top. Per an agreement with her parents, she only rode it to the end of the street, where Noor picked her up in her new ride, a white Corolla a couple years old.

"Heyyyy!" Noor squealed. "I haven't seen you in so long! How are your parents?! How is your brother, is he still fine?!" Noor made a kissy face at Faiza, who laughed as she chucked her board in the back and climbed into the front seat.

"They're all fine, and gross, don't talk about my brother!" Faiza hugged Noor. "Sweet ride, I saw the pics online—I can't believe your dad bought you a car!"

"Yaar, this is his old car, it's not new-new. Still, I'll take it!" She sputtered the car into gear and headed towards the bazaar.

"He lets you drive around without a driver?" In Santa Cruz, her parents always threatened to send her to Pakistan when she talked back. The threat only meant something if girls here couldn't do things girls in Santa Cruz could do. The freedom felt mischievous, like hot gossip in her mouth.

"Well, it's weird. Sometimes he's fine with it, and then sometimes he acts like I haven't been driving around alone and he will insist on coming with me or make me go with Ami. I don't know what his deal is." Noor blew her fringe out of her eyes.

Faiza shook her head and looked out the window. A motorcycle wove around cars. A woman in a powder-blue burka held on to her baby with one arm and the driver with the other as they rocked from one side to the other like a sailboat in the ocean. Noor pulled into the parking lot.

"I'm not sure this shop will have rababs, but they did a few weeks ago when I came by to check out the guitars." Noor spoke straight ahead to the windshield while turning off the car and unbuckling. She had been playing guitar for a couple years, and Faiza watched all the videos Noor posted of herself playing covers online. She was pretty good, Faiza had to admit.

"Sweet. I hope they have really pretty ones. I want one that no one else has." Faiza slammed the car door behind her and hurried to catch up with Noor. Faiza had decided to make the best of her family's move by learning the rabab, the Pukhtun guitar-like instrument she grew up listening to on her mom's cassettes. She didn't know anyone who played it, but in Islamabad there were instructors who might be down to teach an American girl what's up. Her parents were pretty stoked that she wanted to learn more about their culture, even if rababis were usually dudes. She figured it made them reminisce about the last time they lived in Pakistan, what Faiza thought of as "back in the day," before the mullahs had so much power, when playing music was, if not an honorable profession, at least appreciated. Faiza couldn't help but feel like she got a bum deal being born when she was, coming here when they did. This Pakistan seemed less cool than the vintage-jeans-wearing, hippies, hash, and dancing days that she imagined her parents lived through. Not that she knew for sure; she had a feeling though, from occasional comments from aunts and uncles. She'd pore over black-and-white photos dug up online using search words like "vintage Pakistan" and "1960s Pakistan." She'd look at women with heavy eyeliner and bobbed haircuts, short, bell-bottom shalwars, tight kamises with dupattas they wore at the neck instead of covering their breasts, if they wore them at all.

The sleigh bells on the door jingled as they went inside. A standing fan made lazy circles that did nothing to stir the stale, dusty air. Drums—Western kits as well as dholkis and tablas—crowded the back end of the room on worn Persian carpets. Hanging from the ceiling behind the clear plastic counter filled with cassettes and CDs, a few rababs floated like whale bones in a natural history museum, their curved, narrow bellies displayed this way and that to show mother-of-pearl inlays or turquoise stones set in the carved wood. The shopkeeper, a russet-skinned man with a fat Wild-West-style mustache, stood under the rababs as though he was waiting for the girls.

Noor did the talking, since Faiza barely spoke Pashto, much less Urdu. Faiza tried not to look too American by pretending she was shy, moving her head from Noor to the shopkeeper as though she could follow the conversation.

"Faiza, which one do you want?" Noor whispered while looking up at the rababs.

"The prettiest one, the one filled with shells. Ask them if they can carve my name into it. Maybe even do an inlay, with my name. I don't mind paying extra to have one that's specially made for me." Faiza had saved up for this rabab for at least a year, while her parents murmured at home. They watched TV nonstop, news all day, the president talking about a test for Muslims and plans to deport people who had been here for decades. Faiza saved up while her parents worked and worried and argued about what to do.

Noor asked the shopkeeper about getting the name Faiza engraved on the most ornate rabab. He shook his head and launched into a long, one-sided diatribe, while Noor acha, acha'd along with him. Faiza got the gist, that for some reason it couldn't be done. She looked at Noor. Noor nodded her head towards the door so they both turned and walked out to the car.

"What was that about?" Faiza said the minute the glass door shut behind them.

"He said it is not good for a respectable woman to have her name on the rabab." Noor booked it out of there, walking so quickly Faiza trailed behind.

"Wait, why?" Had she done something? Her parents said it was okay. Faiza got in the car as Noor was buckling herself in. Noor put on her sunglasses and started the car.

"So, basically, men would come into the store, and they would see your name, and then maybe they would think of you." Noor hesitated, as though unsure of how exactly to explain the problem to an American girl. "They would know your name..." she paused. "It would be, like, in public."

"Oh." Faiza pretended to understand. She didn't want Noor to think she was dumb. "I see. Yaar, khair de, don't let it bug you. I don't care. Why did we run out? I could have bought one anyway." She didn't want Noor to feel badly, even if this sucked. Faiza felt guilty, like she had exposed herself, like somehow she should have known better.

Kirin Khan

"Nah marra, fuck that guy. We'll get you one somewhere else, I'll ask around." Noor was red-faced, her jaw set.

On the ride home, Faiza tried to imagine what men would get out of knowing her name. Maybe they were so sex-starved they would lie awake at night, mouthing the syllables "Fai-za" to themselves, smitten, with eyes wide and watering in love.

She stared out the window while Noor messed with the CD player, trying to find her favorite songs on *Coke Studio*'s Season 5.

Maybe the men would whisper "Faiza-a-a" while jacking off.

Noor sang along softly to herself. Maybe the men who read her name would shout it when they climaxed, "FAI-ZA!"

Faiza slunk down in her seat so only her eyes could watch out the window. Pale children with light brown hair packed in the back seat of the car next to her stared at her. She raised herself up enough to stick her tongue out at them.

Maybe they'd use her name as a new slang term for a loose woman.

The children gave her cautious smirks—what was it about not smiling in public? Maybe they would use it to blackmail her—they'd find out somehow where she lived, and they would run into her father at work and mention her by name, their familiarity implicating her in something shameful and unclarified. Her dad would flush like an angry Bollywood dad.

"HOW DO YOU KNOW HER NAME?!" he'd yell, all bloodshot eyes and quivering jowls.

Faiza watched as a mule-drawn cart ran alongside them, piled high with what looked like long grass. She wasn't sure what it was for.

Her name, in public. Her nascent reputation would be ruined, her family ashamed. But how on earth could they actually do anything, with just her all-too-common first name to go off of? Something about it needled her brain.

Noor dropped Faiza off at her driveway. Faiza carried her skateboard inside with a half-hearted "Khuda hafiz."

Two days passed. Faiza stayed in her room, occasionally standing out on the balcony to hear the azaan and watch people walk the perimeter of the park across the street. She hid, practiced being an unseen woman, a private-room woman. Her parents knew something was up; they talked to her in softer tones and didn't ask her to help as much.

On the third day, when Faiza emerged from her dark bedroom for evening che, Mom was half asleep, reclining on the sofa. "Bache, what's wrong with you? You're acting like a beat dog. Or have you become very religious now? You know you don't need to do purdah from your own parents."

Faiza added a teaspoon of sugar to her tea and stirred it. "Some man said I couldn't get my name on the rabab because it'd make me a whore or something."

Mom barked a laugh and put down her tea cup. "What? What are you talking about—"

"Cuz you know, guys would learn my name." Was this not a thing? Why didn't her mom know why already? Why didn't her mom warn her before?

"Wait, who is this man to tell you what you can have?" She sat up and started gesturing with her hands as she talked, working herself up. "Who is he to us?"

She didn't let Faiza answer as she ranted about his nerve, and then she changed gears and turned to Faiza. "Kha, so some idiot dokander tells you what to do now? Is that right?" She looked fiery and powerful, her dark eyes glowed. "I thought you were a Pukhtuna. I thought I raised you to be a fighter."

Faiza stayed quiet, ashamed.

"Call your cousin. No one is meant to stay at home all day like a potted plant, Faizo."

Faiza loved the way her family sweetened her name from "Faiza" to "Faizo," so their lips made a kiss shape at the end of it. Pukhtuns were known as warriors, but what about these little kisses?

Faiza got up, downed the last bit of over-sweet tea, and marched to her room to get dressed. Who was he to tell her where she could put her name? Some sad little boys might get excited? Pathetic. She threw on a clean shalwar kameez and called Noor while tying her sneakers.

"Where have you been?" Noor sounded annoyed.

"I know, I know, I'm sorry. Listen, you up for an adventure?"

"Adventure?" Noor's curiosity was always her weak spot. "Sounds good. What's up?"

"Just meet me at the end of my street in twenty minutes." Faiza thought for a sec. "Oh! And wear tennis shoes. We might need to run."

After hanging up, Faiza packed her satchel. She wrapped her pens in the pink plastic bags she got whenever she bought snacks at the knick-knack and drugstore shop downtown. Opening her dresser drawer, she lingered over two pairs of gloves left over from her "full coverage" phase. Faiza's rough hands snagged the heavy fabric. She tossed the gloves in her bag and scanned the drawer for the rest. Faiza smiled to herself and grabbed two abayas shaped like black lab coats and two dark scarves. Her bag stuffed and arms overflowing with cloth, she rushed out the door while throwing on one of the abayas, shifting the bag and fabric to get her arms in one sleeve and then the other. She reached Noor's car with the front of it still open, looking wildly disheveled, a mad scientist.

"Ummm hiiii." Noor stretched her syllables long to make it clear she was puzzled by Faiza's fashion statement today. "What. Are. You. Wearing."

"Ha! Look I know it looks weird, but just trust me. Put this on, this one's for you." She shoved the cloth in Noor's lap as she got in the front seat. Using the rearview mirror, Faiza slipped on her scarf the way she used to wear it in Sunday school, complete with a little safety pin on the inside holding it closed just under her chin. "This way no one will look at us. Two nice girls, nothing too exciting."

"Okay, sure. This is part of the adventure, I take it." Noor clicked into full ride-or-die sidekick mode. She threw the navy-blue scarf over her head and shifted into gear. Faiza remembered why they had always been besties. "Where to?"

"The music store."

By the time they reached the parking lot, the sun had gone down completely. The parking lot was nearly empty—this particular square didn't stay open late, although others would be well lit through the entire night in case anyone came by for late night fruit, chips, or paracetamol. Noor parked a few spaces away from the sole street lamp. She slipped into her abaya, buttoning it up as much as she could before getting out of the car to fasten the lower snaps. Faiza handed her a pair of long black gloves.

"You're not serious." Noor snatched the gloves and shook them at Faiza.

"Oh, but I am."

"What next, niqab?"

"If I had one, you'd be wearing it! Trust me, the more coverage, the better!" Faiza laughed. "This will have to do."

Fully dressed in her black abaya, navy-blue hijab, and black gloves, Noor looked looked like any devout Muslimah, the loose-fitting overcoat hiding the shape of her body. Outside the streetlight's halo, she looked like a shadow.

Faiza slung her bag over her shoulder, and they walked slowly to the shop where they had looked for rababs. The shop was closed, a sheet-metal door pulled down and locked to a hook set in the concrete sidewalk. Faiza stared at the metal door; her gloved hand reached inside her bag and pulled out two fat paint pens.

"Are you sure you want to do this?" Noor looked uncertain, the doubt in her face made her seem younger.

"Totally. It's gonna be sweet." Faiza grinned and squared her shoulders, trying to look as confident and bro-y as dudes always seemed to whenever they were about to do stupid shit. Faiza handed a gold paint marker to Noor. The marker was fatter than those little-kid crayons, the ones for tiny hands that don't care about coloring inside the lines.

"You will get me in trouble." Noor smiled back, not quite convinced. She uncapped the marker, and the fumes made her wince. "What will we write?"

Faiza ignored her, pried the cap off between her teeth and immediately started a huge Arabic-looking outline on the door, checking something written on her hand to get the letters right. The slick black paint looked like vinyl and dripped down here and there, like tears, like blood, like the ways a body shows what's inside to the outside—pain, a wound, all of it trickled, all of it reflected moon and streetlight.

"What does that say?" Noor tried sounding it out. "Are you sure that's right?"

"It's supposed to say 'da peyghlo vaar dey'—like 'the girls are hitting back,' or 'it's our time now,' depending on how you read it, but I don't know if I spelled it right. I used Google Translate," Faiza confessed.

"You what?!" Noor coughed to hide her laughter, to avoid drawing attention from anyone who might still be out, but her eyes watered with the effort.

"Hey! I can't read or write Pukhto at all, don't laugh!" Faiza made a faux-hurt face and shushed her. In a harsh whisper, she blurted, "I just feel like, I want to let people know that we're out here, like flashing the Bat-Signal or something. Watch your back, we comin' for ya."

"Great, so they will know Google-Translate-Pukhtunas are here. Good job, we're all quivering! Most of them can't read Pukhto anyway!" Noor drew a flower in the corner with gold petals.

"Whatever. We'll show them. They can read this." Faiza wrote underneath the phrase in huge, swooping letters that could be seen by any men driving cars on the street, any men who might come by tonight or tomorrow, so large and shiny they would see it behind their eyelids when they closed them:

Her name.

Alycia Pirmohamed

LETTER TO MY BODY

Because forgetting is like puncturing a vein, letting the blood
out, hiding the body away. I am not that kind
of criminal. I keep my dark with me, carry it so deeply
it calcifies into black starling and birch eye,
a harebell's shadow pressed against afternoon earth.
I am pulled toward the clay and harden in it.
I try to remember the rules for telling a body you will love it infinitely.
I tell my body I will hold it like a looking glass against the night.
Tell it *yes*, there is a way to reflect those constellations
that live in the dark against the dark.

Alycia Pirmohamed

WE HAVE THE ENDINGS

Every story is like this

new blood,
ivy leaf,
black thrush, open mouth,
stitched lace, elegy.

I hate to know the endings first.

I hate to know that moonlight wrings pigeons
away

and that the view from the balcony
is clay-fired light and mountains.

We are prism-ed
to this point, cliff-edged,

we are seeds pointed inward,
we are an arrangement

of stars.

We are integers,
whole and negative
all at once,

Graffiti

second-generation mixed drinks,
blurred lines, missteps, clipped wings.

I live inside
a body I sometimes wish
to unclaim,

to set afloat in the river, embalmed
in a cotton white sari,

petal-ing off fabric, unwinding
in the current
like film.
Every story is like this thunderstorm,

rising action, rain, ninety-degree light—
a woman's woman
planting an apple seed,

and earth that refuses to grow
her anything.

Alycia Pirmohamed

TWISTED WOOD

And you are the obscenity.
The dark. The slippage. The wreckage.

The full stop.

Disclaimer: I am now beyond the tree line,
the spine line—

I have arrived at the overexposed edge
and its arrangement of white hanging cliffs.

Tell me. What haven't you crushed already?

Allah, a spot of blood on the moon.
Or the moon as a bomb and Allah exploding

into a roughage of stars.

And you are the shrapnel,
and you have landed on every vertebrae.

This is the fruit you have cut open and left to rust.

This is the world you have conjured—inferno,
where all of the endings are flawed

and we have run out of beginnings.

Ramy El-Etreby

MY LIFE IS A TAPESTRY

My life has been a tapestry of rich and royal hue,
An everlasting vision of the ever-changing view,
A wondrous woven magic in bits of blue and gold,
A tapestry to feel and see, impossible to hold.

—Carole King

I imagine myself to be a tapestry, attached to a magical loom, holding tension in a warp of threads, running lengthwise, perpetually expanding. I am a collection of strings, constantly woven and entangled in a woof, running crosswise. I am ever-growing, made up of countless fibers, glorious and rich, dyed in many colors, crafting one vibrant story after the next, vivid and complex, a narrative so intricate it would take a lifetime to track every fibrous thread and try to unweave them all.

Exquisitely designed with a multitude of threads. Each one can be felt to the touch. The hours of labor put in by the artist. Every string runs between the fingers of the weaver before it's meticulously woven into place. Every tapestry has a living physical memory embedded in its fibers.

For this journal, I was asked to write about graffiti. I could not. I was at a loss for words. Graffiti just does not speak to me. Not like tapestries do. Tapestries are grand and abundant. The intricacy of the details. The numerous stories being told. The lushness, the romance, the drama.

Graffiti, unlike tapestries, has no tactile fibers with memories existing in them. Graffiti stays superficial, while tapestries run deep. A tapestry boasts complexity and tells multiple narratives. A graffito is simple and only tells one. A graffito offers no physical connection. A graffito does not distinguish itself from the surface it covers in any tangible way. It always shows up flat and two-dimensional.

Graffiti often feels hurried. Not fully thought through before it is executed. It manifests through powerful sprays of paint, thrown up quickly and covertly. I don't typically understand the messages being sent. Whatever the messages are, they never seem meant for me.

While graffiti speaks a language I don't always understand, I can recognize the value it has in modern society. When the messages being passed from the artist to the public are immediate and relevant to the here and now, graffiti can be powerful and inspiring. When used as a rogue vehicle for public communication, for expressing the socio-political issues of the day, graffiti can be galvanizing and agitating.

Graffiti gets political. Graffiti gets controversial. Whether it's livening up the deathly wall separating the modern state of Israel from the occupied Palestinian lands, or flourishing across the crumbling wall that once split Berlin and the rest of Germany in half, graffiti tells the story of the people living on the land at the time. Graffiti is the sharing of hurt and angry voices in the public sphere. Graffiti is an act of democracy. Graffiti is an act of freedom.

Graffiti stretches back thousands of years to the days of ancient Egypt and the Greeks and the Romans. The hieroglyphics that can still be seen today etched on sandstone walls throughout the Nile River Valley are some of the earliest examples of graffiti known to humankind. The fact that these etchings still exist in their original state makes graffiti one of the oldest visual art forms that is still practiced today.

Egypt is the land of my ancestors, and, for that reason alone, I should feel more connected to the hieroglyphics. If it is a part of my historical DNA, then it should bring out a special reverence within me. Yet, curiously, I don't feel particularly connected to those ancient

Ramy El-Etreby

etchings that fill my mother's land. Like modern graffiti, the hiero-glyphics appear a little too flat for me, too muted in their details. I simply don't understand the messages.

I might not speak the language of my ancestors, but I do know how to connect to them through their most dramatic of expressions. With so many theatrical artifacts I can look to, I just don't have the time for the hieroglyphics. I much prefer to see the Great Pyramids of Giza or the Great Sphinx, none of which are flat or muted. These are the most dramatic relics of the ancient world. Show me a statue of Ramses II standing eleven meters tall and weighing eighty-three tons, and I will shiver and quiver. Show me the painted limestone bust of Nefertiti or a pharaoh's coffin exquisitely plastered in gold and countless other colors, and I may cry, or squeal, or faint.

I am a theatre artist. Theatre is my one true love. I always live for the drama. Nothing is more exciting to me than live performance. The theatre bug first bit me when I was cast in a musical during my freshman year of high school. *Little Shop of Horrors.* A musical about a man-eating plant! Ever since then, drama has been the only language I can truly understand. I'll take in a live theatre performance any day of the week. Give me a satirical comedy on Friday night and a violent tragedy on Saturday. Show me a farce and then show me a melodrama. The more heightened the stakes are, the better. If there's a break into song and dance, I am absolutely here for it. Show me some "Sturm und Drang" and some "schadenfreude," and I will shake and stir. I will weep happy tears. I will laugh through the pain. I want to feel all the feelings all the time. I will emote and exhaust myself, leaving my heart bleeding on the theatre floor.

I live in Los Angeles, arguably one of the most dramatic cities in the world. There is a reason why the film and TV industry thrives out here. The Art Deco remains of the 1920s and '30s provide the perfect backdrop for ghosts of Hollywood past to haunt the city, remembering an opulence that has been gathering dust and is slowly withering away. The geography and climate alone is epic and ripe for height-ened storytelling. The unwavering warm and sunny weather; the breathtaking sunsets over the golden coastline; the rugged, dusty mountains bisecting the city; the twisty, curvy canyon roads like Laurel Canyon and Mulholland Drive; the marvelous homes hidden in little pockets off those same canyon roads, coexisting alongside coyotes and mountain lions. There's this constant threat of destruction. The raging wildfires with clouds of ash raining down on us all; the massive earthquakes that will swallow us all; the apocalyptic traffic jams that trap us all; the dry, parched land that begs for rain; and the blessed rain itself that makes us all freak out when it finally comes.

Every day, a cast of characters transforms this city of angels into a frenzy of kooky pseudo-celebrity personalities. Just the other night, a hot-pink Corvette zipped past me on the road. It was a Sunday night at 10 PM, and, while most people were at home in bed asleep, that speed demon was living their best life. In a town of four million people, I instantly knew that the driver was Angelyne, the busty, blonde billboard queen of the 1980s, a bona fide local celebrity running the streets. Is there anything more dramatic than a blonde bombshell way past her prime but still doing the most? There's truly no place like home.

I try to remind myself that everybody is different. Not everyone appreciates all that drama. Some people prefer a quieter, simpler kind of life, far from the kooks and angel-headed hipsters that crawl across urban metropolises like LA, and that's perfectly fine. For them, maybe they respond better to graffiti rather than live performance. To each their own. We are diverse, and that's what keeps things fresh and exciting. There is something out there for everyone. I may prefer a complex tapestry with countless threads telling one dramatic story after the next, but I can also push myself to appreciate graffiti and its simplicity more. We don't always have the luxury of time and space for complexity. If all we had time for was a quick glance, then graffiti would be the winner. It's a cliché, but sometimes less really is more.

I wonder, if I were a graffito and I only had one message to share with the public, what would I say? How can I take my complicated self and simplify it, but still retain my essence? I would ideally be on the exterior wall of a historic theatre in Los Angeles and would obviously say something theatre-related. I would be dramatic and witty, and maybe a little campy and ironic. Perhaps I would be a stencil of William Shakespeare, wearing full drag, face beat to the gods with lashes and a giant wig, with a long cigarette holder dangling from his hands and a chat cloud above him saying something like, "What were you expecting, darling? Shakespeare?"

Gary Dauphin

SUICIDE JACQ

A woman barrels up Alvarado Street, sun flashing off the top of her sweat-slick, bald head. Olympic, James M. Woods, back to Olympic, back to Woods, Eighth. Her body and its associated hashtags are trending north, this even when circumstance forces her to double back or she's dancing upstream on Alvarado's southbound side. She blasts through red signals and clambers over the hot hoods of idling cars. She pinballs off bumpers and hops onto curbs to slalom lampposts and parking meters. She lights up all four lanes—six if you count the sidewalks. There, she does equally death-defying work avoiding collisions with LA's working men and women, with their varied ways of making do. She vaults the ad-hoc grocery aisles they've set up on milk crates, darts through their tightly packed and likely unlicensed swap meets. She long-jumps square yards of DVDs and jeans laid out on neat blue tarps, leaping entire sectors of the informal economy with every bound. A thing to behold, half of Los Angeles says. To which the other half rejoins: Suicide Jacq is not a thing!

In addition to the human obstacle course, Jacq's near-daily performances feature guest stars and amplifiers. The guest stars started chasing her around Olympic today: first two cops, then three, then four. A black-and-white is northbound on Alvarado, too, play-by-playing the chase until the helicopters can get there. Unless you have a police scanner, the amplifiers are your go-to, real-time channel, Jacq's

Graffiti

POC United

appearances in a given part of town documented on all the standard platforms via check-in, selfie and WTF??!-style update. #suicidejacq #jacqlives #jacqnotjack #freedomformothers. The invisible meridians she follows across the city exert magnetic effects on all nearby phones and their cameras.

The webs think Jacq is increasingly playing to the cameras, "what next?" guiding her movements as much as "where next?" For example: jammed onto the east side of Alvarado between Eighth and Seventh this time of day is a thicket of food carts. Jacq dives right in, when the prudent route would take her left or right onto a relatively unobstructed Seventh Street. Instead, she takes a sort of food crawl, slowing to smack her lips at churros and bacon dogs, to unwrap and juggle a tamal into her mouth like a sea lion tossing a fish, to triple bend at the waist to sniff at chili'd and limed mango in a manner unto a herky-jerky living gif. She gives a proffered bomb pop an exaggerated no-no-no-no (hot take: THE RUMORS ARE TRUE!!) and snatches up several Spanish limes née mamoncillos near the end of the block, popping and sucking and spitting out the pits in what later analysis will judge to have been one seamless motion. A non-thing to behold, indeed!

All those phones point as much at the world as at Jacq, so they also capture one early afternoon assignation between married hand-holders unmarried to each other (#BUSTED!), one grey-market oxycodone deal (#BUSTED!), one teenage runaway long believed either dead or trafficked (#FOUND!), and many, many, many violations of the City of Los Angeles's street food code (#UGH #YUCK #SALMONELLA). The social web also managed to do a solid for one poor slob when it recorded Jacq pausing for a precious split-second to ¯_(ツ)_/¯ at a red tub of what the comments would later describe as Southern (a.k.a. Very Black) potato salad. Because who the fuck sells Southern, mustard-style potato salad this far north of South LA, butting all the way up against MacArthur Park? #businessplanfail. #potatosaladguy. But lemons into sweet, overly sweetened lemonade: he'd be on the Food Channel in mere days.

Let's be clear that, while our running woman is one of Los Angeles's dwindling cohort of African American residents, she's happily wrapped herself in the whole of her city's ethnic tapestry. For example, Suicide Jacq never passes up the chance for centrifugal, how-do-you-do twirls with any abuelas she might happen upon, Chinese and Korean grannies too. And yes: one or two bulky purses have gone arcing like hammers on Olympic-grade throws as a result. But this wasn't the meadow in Silver Lake, where a stroller had reportedly tumbled in her wake. Unreported was that she'd tumbled with it, getting both arms under the towheaded tyke involved before it could kiss concrete. Because she's fast, our Suicide Jacq. Fast, and strong, too.

The abuelas always say the same thing once they've recovered their purses, not ¿Jacq, cómo pudiste? ¿Cómo pudiste hacerlo? but: ¡Jacq, cuidado! De seguro esta ves, la policía te va matar! (Or thereabouts as she understood it. Her Korean and Chinese were even worse—i.e., nonexistent—but she assumed they were telling her much the same.)

Jacq laughs in response, flashes that toothy, screen-ready smile. Tells the old ladies not to worry, that her show won't be cancelled just yet. It'd been "The Summer of Jacq," and the whole city seemed to genuinely want the party to keep going. A weekday, Jacq-themed pop-up had breathed new life into *The Sentinel*, two folded sheets (eight pages) asking and answering "Where's Jacq?" to the best of their ability. You could win ninety-two bucks and thirty cents if you were the first to call in to Real 92.3 with a sighting. Every day there were more t-shirts for sale in Leimert Park Plaza emblazoned with variations on RUN JACQ! RUN! and FREE JACQ! and FREEDOM FOR MOTHERS (JACQ), her face floating in the center. Even the August heat seemed to bend to her will, with days on which she appeared cooler than those she didn't, easier on the crowds. Angelenos of every stripe got goose pimples when Jacq flew by, because they knew something wonderful and strange was happening, with more strange and wonderful to come. Takes doubled, necks rubbered, every mouth formed a neat "O!" around sharp inhalations. City blocks yet to be set in a direct uproar by her started vibrating long before there was even a rumor she was coming their way. Even people who didn't believe the stories—cynical, story-drunk citizens of LaLaLand!—had to admit they could hear a good story coming. They couldn't avoid wondering how that story (if not actual facts) would play out today.

Today, today, today: how is Suicide Jacq going to die today?

Here's what the police say happened:

At or around eleven AM, Jacqueline Watson, twenty-six years old, five feet, eight inches, female, Black, born Los Angeles County, charged with murder, unlawful flight to avoid prosecution, child abduction, and child endangerment, was spotted by two LAPD officers as she made her way westbound on Olympic at Bonnie Brae. After conferring and confirming their identification, the two officers approached Watson, who immediately fled. They pursued her west along Olympic and then north up Alvarado, where they were joined by two other officers and a nearby patrol car.

Given this fugitive's tendency to flee on foot and in commandeered vehicles, and also given her clear disregard for the safety of those around her, officers have specific guidance to contain her while maintaining a safe perimeter. Everyone is asked to remember that every single automobile pursuit involving Watson has ended with her deliberately, catastrophically crashing her car. There have been reports of gunfire in her vicinity; several houses she's taken refuge in have burned down. Sensational stories may get you clicks, but it's a miracle no one has died.

Watson was wearing jeans, a black hooded sweatshirt and bright yellow running shoes. As during previous encounters, she was also wearing headphones. White, clamshell-style this time.

The LAPD views the suspect as a clear danger to the public, but also to herself and to her daughter. Although today's incident was a foot chase, in four blocks she managed to jump over a dozen parked cars, damaging several. She disrupted traffic, knocked a number of people off the sidewalk, and caused minor injury to several, including two elderly women.

No, we don't understand how she got out of the area, either.

This is what the immigrants say happened:

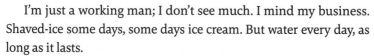

I'm just a working man; I don't see much. I mind my business. Shaved-ice some days, some days ice cream. But water every day, as long as it lasts.

Yes, I saw the black woman running. It's not a big park so you would know I was lying if I said something else. I saw her and I saw the police chasing her. I keep to the green around the lake, that's where there are people with money. People walking or exercising or pushing strollers. The rest of the park is poor unfortunates lying down. Lazy men and men not right with God.

I will tell you what I told the other officer. I didn't want you to catch her. She seemed happy. After she passed, I got down on my knees and prayed for the Lord to deliver her to his justice, which is not always yours. I know you say she did something, but the police say everyone did something.

Did I tell you she looked at me? When she ran by. She smiled at me. All her hair is cut off like a man's but my heart stopped because she reminded me of a Black American actress whose videos were popular when I was a boy. I can't remember what that actress's name is, but I know God heard my prayer today. I thank him for getting her away from you.

This is what the homeless had to say:

You getting off me? Won't talk unless you get off me.

Yeah, I saw her. Saw you all, too. I make it a point to know where you all are all of the time. For safety.

You know where I live. Tent's on Wilshire, little west of Alvarado. Was until today and all this. And it better be there when I get back!

I wouldn't be old as I am if I was the kind to miss that kind of commotion. Saw her running round the lake like I said, you all chasing plain as day. She comes all the way round then hops the little wall that keeps the sidewalk on Wilshire separate from the park. She was there in the tents with us for a spell, too, until you all started getting too close. Then she looks at me and gives me The Nod, which I appreciated because young people in Los Angeles do not give proper respect anymore. Me, I'd have kept running if I was her, run the hell away. But she stops and nods and then she jumps into the street. Not jumps. Tumbles, cartwheels, rolls? All that to the middle of Alvarado and Wilshire.

Course I never seen nothing like it. You ever seen anything like it? Stop asking me if I'm high. Not under stress, either. No more than any other day, at least.

You gonna let me go now? What about just getting off me then?

I saw traffic coming towards her in both directions on Wilshire. I saw her in the middle of the street and a bunch of cops coming for the kill—come on now, you know I'm not resisting—I saw cars and I saw people. People on bicycles and people walking and people watching. I saw cop cars running east after her on Wilshire hard and regular cars coming toward her from all four ways, I saw those taxis that aren't taxis honking and trying not to get stuck, I saw her—get off me—and you all and a bus, I saw a bus—I said don't—

Okay, okay, okay. We're all cool.

I saw the bus hit her. The 720.

I saw it hit her with these eyes. Not just me, everybody there did including you all. Why don't you ask all the other police that was there what happened instead of bothering me? They saw her go into the street, just like I did, saw her dodge one, two, three cars, then, instead of sidestepping what gets her, saw her jump in front and plant. Arms open like she's waiting for a hug. We all heard it, too. They heard that bus hitting her all the way on San Pedro.

Bus driver jammed on the brakes and the bus did a little skid. Then just like that there are more police cars up around the bus and you all are everywhere. Some of you kneeling next to the bus, others doing crowd control—which is just people control. Police shouting into radios, shouting at each other, yelling for vehicles and people on the sidewalk to move.

I don't move because this is where I live. The crowd gets bigger and starts pushing against you all while you all push back. Someone up on top of a bus stop starts yelling "JACQ! JACQ! JACQ!" over and over.

I don't know how many ways I can tell you to get off me.

No. I was there. I've been there since I was a kid. I've seen it all. Including seeing a bald-headed sister get herself hit by a bus today.

Gary Dauphin

Saw her get picked up by the bike rack and tossed up in the air. Saw her spin head over heels and hit the windshield, hit the bike rack again before getting plowed under.

I saw it, the whole thing, plain as day, and then I un-saw it because she wasn't there after all that.

Jacq came back to the world—this side of it, at least—in stutters and slips.

First nothing, then silence, then a not-silence that wasn't sound but her own, wordless, animal thinking. Then thinking with words: thank you, thank you, thank you. Gratitude she had an un-crushed and un-fractured skull to enclose all that thinking and thanking.

After that, several things happened at once. Three memories like sharp slaps to the face: her name, her daughter's name, and what it felt like to be run down by a bus. Localized memories of pain strobed in her left arm, left leg, right leg, and right arm in quick succession. From there she picked her way through sensations that took a while to identify as exterior, as not-Jacq. The feel of shredded and torn fabric below her with grit and asphalt below that. Of heat coming down from above.

Jacq's ears popped, and she could hear a large engine idling. The smell of burning motor oil and gasoline and rubber pricked at her nostrils and she sneezed. She was 100% clear that she was a living, breathing woman rather than a smudge under a bus when she heard clapping. Two pairs of hands. One pair was steady and grown-up and desultory, the other tiny and fast, its pace the fluttering of a small bird's wings.

Jacq smiled, said her daughter's name aloud to herself to make sure she could speak. She sat up to look around, got maybe three inches before her forehead hit hot metal.

"Try opening your eyes first," someone shouted, laughing and unhelpful.

The undercarriage of the bus vibrated just above Jacq's nose. If she twisted her neck, she could see pieces of a phone and headphones trailing away towards the bus's front. Edging up against the bus in all directions were the wheels and bumpers of what she counted as three police cars. She was lying roughly in the middle of its footprint. The vehicles were idling, too, although one seemed to have smashed into another before both smashed into the bus's flank. The third police car nosed a bit under the bus's rear like a dog trying to nudge its owner. All those engines—bus included—strained at each other, their combined energies summing up to new trajectories. Jacq realized the bus was inching forward and that its back wheels would reach her face if she waited long enough. Like it wanted to run her down all over again, but right this time. With intention.

She picked a direction at random and shimmied out into wan sunlight. She stood and stretched, dusted herself off. From there, she did a quick 360.

Wilshire Boulevard and Alvarado Street spread out around her like an evacuated movie set, Jacq its only actor. Every other living thing had been sent home for the day, except for a few stray squirrels and birds screeching in panic, and all the plants. Closer inspection of the resulting film would have revealed that the traffic lights and stores to the east were all dark. If anything moved or gave off light, it was thanks to a self-contained power source—gasoline, propane, batteries. The life left to a warm body.

The sun hung smaller and higher in the sky than normal, giving off underpowered light that was more fluorescent than solar.

Grocery bags, cell phones, pocketbooks, backpacks—even LAPD service revolvers—littered the sidewalks and streets nearest Jacq, little piles of personal effects sitting on beds of shoes, pants, under-garments, shirts, hats. The piles marked the locations of people Jacq remembered seeing gaping at her earlier. The scene after she crossed over always reminded her of a B-movie where a mad scientist's zap gun has turned every adult into a baby, their little feet kicking above oversized clothes. Only without the mad scientist, zap gun, babies, or B-movie. Farther along Wilshire and Alvarado, the streets were simi-larly littered, but with the added complication of cars, empty sets of clothes in the driver's seats. Many of these cars formed precarious piles of their own, the force of their collisions spent and their previously held attributes—speed, orientation the moment Jacq died under the bus—difficult to determine.

Jacq knew from previous jumps that the farther away she went from her personal ground zero, the fewer piles she would find, all of it fading away at a radius of about five hundred feet. Beyond the rough circumference where the piles and smoking cars stopped, there'd only be dated-seeming architecture and shriveled trees. The only parts of the city just outside that five-hundred-foot radius not bled to gray would be the path Jacq had run to her encounter with the bus, back around the lake, down Alvarado, left on Olympic. That route would be as rich with color and detritus as the intersection, as if the city was a coloring book and only those parts most recently alive to her and her presence had merited filling-in.

Jacq noticed two live humans standing across the street near the Westlake / MacArthur Park Metro station. It'd been particularly crowded there when the bus hit her and the two figures were walled-in by tall piles of clothes, by makeshift stands piled with groceries and fruit. Columns of t-shirts hung on poles lined up behind the pair, banners from a medieval reenactment. Jacq's own face looked down at her from one.

Both figures were wearing bulky earmuffs. The taller figure was a long, lean woman whose copper dreads swept down a little too picture-perfectly when she took her earmuffs off. The smaller one was a girl, her earmuffs set in a nimbus of lively curls. The girl was doing a very good job of clapping and hiding her eyes behind one forearm at the same time.

Jacq waved at her daughter, mimed taking something off her head. The girl responded by taking her headphones off while jumping up and down. She shot sly looks out from behind her arm.

"Mommy's back," said Jacq. Her daughter's name was Joy.

It was the tall slip of a woman who replied. "Yes, you are." Her name was Nadege.

The three stood there. The two grown-ups avoided each other's eyes by grinning at the girl. The girl played peek-a-boo with her mother.

Joy broke first.

"What did you bring me back?" she blurted.

"I hope someone out here was wearing my shade," Nadege muttered. She scanned the ground. Her eyes were almost as greedy as the girl's even as she took hold of Joy's hand to keep her back.

Jacq re-eyed the smashed cars on Wilshire. Tendrils of gasoline were reaching for a smoldering hot dog grill down Alvarado. The smoke floated straight up into the sky, undisturbed by wind or breeze.

"Why don't you let Mommy clean up here," she said. "I think I saw a video game store around Alvarado and Seventh."

Joy disappeared down the sidewalk. Nadege stayed put to give the intersection long, sideways looks.

"Another mess," Nadege decided. "How'd you come over this time? Shoot yourself in the head? Slit your throat? Blow up a paddle boat?"

Jacq nodded back towards the 720. "Pow. Right in the kisser."

"Nice. That's definitely going to make the papers over there."

"TV, too, I figure."

"The others aren't going to be happy."

"If the others were ever gonna be happy, they wouldn't have killed themselves."

Fresh memories of pain went from her limbs to her spine then up her neck into her skull. She remembered rooting herself to the ground and squaring to face the bus. How she'd claimed the impact, quashing natural instincts toward self-preservation.

"You want your fucking lipstick, or what?" Jacq barked. But Nadege was already gone.

Jacq found Nadege and Joy almost exactly where she'd entered the park at Seventh and Alvarado. They'd assembled a minor echo of the homeless encampment exactly one block north. Joy sprawled on her back in the mouth of a tent—Jacq frowned, imagining lice and worse—staring at a handheld video game. A semicircle of food carts and coolers faced the tent. Nadege fussed with the grills there, her back to Joy, double- and triple-cooking salvaged meats and empanadas.

Over to one side sat several tarps layered with the fruit of the pair's own explorations. Their efforts had been more practical than Jacq might have previously allowed, the pair paying sustained (collaborative?) attention to clothes. The adults' and children's outfits laid on the tarps were brighter and girlier than the tomboyish uniform Jacq usually selected for her daughter and herself. The realization set hot, liquid panic running through her.

"You good, Joy?" Jacq asked. She stopped on the extreme edge of the makeshift picnic, hanging there as if worried Nadege and Joy could banish her from its polite society. "You eat?"

Joy grunted an answer. Her mother dithered for a few beats before allowing herself the day's first real rest on a nearby bench. She lay down and stared up at a featureless sky, listening to the sounds her daughter and Nadege made. The other woman brought over a takeout plate laden with food, laying it on the bench above Jacq's head. She didn't bother getting vertical to eat, reaching over to take half-blind stabs with a plastic fork.

Her body was un-injured, but she was in pain in those places where recollection and sensation could be plausibly confused. Like her teeth, which she was sure still ached at the roots from having been knocked out of her mouth. Headaches were a constant here, but her vision strobed unpredictably with retinal flashes she'd last remembered seeing when the bones in her face had exploded. The muscles in her back burned at the remembered insults, awful sideways postures.

"I could lie up here forever," Jacq said, looking to redirect her interior monologue. She looked over in Nadege's direction for help, but it was Joy who responded first this time. The girl rolled to her stomach and started smashing the game in her hand into pieces like a caveman beating the ground with a bone.

"Joy!" said Nadege without looking over. "Hey!" She held the hot dogs with tongs, jabbing the meat at an unrelated direction for emphasis. "You won't get nice things if you're going to break them."

"Nice? I have two of that game already." Then: "It's boring here."

"Yes, baby," said her mother, tendons popping in her neck.

"I want ice cream. I want to go home."

Jacq sat bolt upright. Whenever Joy said the word "home," she responded as if the girl meant the apartment building they shared with Nadege, this even as she assumed down to the marrow of her recently shattered bones that the girl meant something else. Jacq nodded, nodded, nodded. Nodded some more.

"I can get you ice cream," she said. There was a convenience store down Alvarado, and if she ran, she might be able to get to there in time to salvage something from its freezer. Tomorrow she'd have to kill herself and get some new games.

People think no one knows what happens to the dead, but that's only partially true. Suicides know what happens to some other suicides. People who died passively, unawares, or unwillingly left corpses; those who killed themselves and didn't flinch, who didn't turn away from their deaths the whole way down, those people woke up whole, healed, and unhurt where Jacq, Joy, and Nadege were. The rules also worked in reverse: kill yourself here, don't flinch, and you were back where you started.

The place didn't have a name, but then it wasn't clear it was an actual place to begin with. What was known was that nothing would grow reliably here except people, who aged at a slightly faster clip than people remembered aging. Plants survived, but required constant, professional-grade attention. There were no birds, fish, insects, or animals that hadn't come over with a person and, like those people, they were neuters. If you managed to catch flesh that had been here for a while and eat it, it was indistinct, flavorless.

Everything was like that here. There were no definite qualities to "here" except for suicides and their issues and whatever was in their immediate surroundings when they closed their eyes on the other side. Here was a map constantly being scribbled over by depressives and the terminally ill, a zone in perpetual danger of revision by the next jumper. Dig a ditch, paint a masterpiece, set furniture out front of Hancock Park's biggest mansion, and if someone crossed over within five hundred feet of your handiwork, it disappeared, that which had been yours replaced by someone else's things. Architectural eras jammed up against each other depending on when the last person had died nearby. Where no one had ever taken their life, a hazy, generic blanket of grey grass bled towards a vague horizon. Who could give a place like that a name?

Practical concerns had Jacq labeling where they were "Here" for Joy, where they came from "There." She was adamant that they were, in no way, shape, or form, in heaven, hell, limbo, or purgatory. What kind of prison left the front door open for anyone to get out the way they'd come in? Home was always a head injury away.

Jacq also knew Here wasn't hell because her daughter was with her. Joy was seven years old in a place that, by all accounts, had never seen a pregnancy or a birth, where the closest thing to a child was quiet-eyed teenagers who had crossed over in the wake of their own traumas, swallowing fistfuls of pills or slitting their wrists.

Joy was innocent of all that, but she was Here all the same. Jacq knew that her daughter unnerved people here, no small feat in a ghost town full of suicides. People looked at Joy with sad, aghast eyes and fixed Jacq with accusing stares. Suicides are forgiving by temperament and circumstance, but most people seemed to have decided that if they got too close to either Jacq or Joy they'd have to ask exactly how the girl had gotten Here, whether she was in further danger.

Jacq couldn't blame them. She asked the same questions all the time. But Joy was Here, and no answer Jacq could come up with would undo what had been done There, at least not yet. All she could do was keep jumping across the abyss—jumping, jumping, never flinching. Keep the refrigerator full and cold, the power on and the DVDs and games new. Keep jumping for Joy, Jacq had told herself more than once as she'd crossed over, wincing at the pun. Keep jumping until Joy could jump for herself and save them both.

Jacq and Joy live in a loft just north of Leimert Park Plaza. On the other side, it's a big, bright knot of rooms that an acquaintance of Jacq's lives in, a tall, pretty bartender whose parents pay her rent and keep her in tall, pretty heels. Jacq admired the unencumbered ease of her life There, how empty it was, just bartending and playing at painting. Once the realities and perks of life Here had become clear to her, Jacq had claimed the apartment. She found Nadege living down the hall, a rare circumstance given the lack of density Here, the endless available real estate.

When they got back to the apartment, Nadege helped Jacq bring all her bags up, items collected from the corner where she'd crossed over. Jacq reciprocated with Nadege's haul and then loitered in her kitchen. Nadege hugged Joy once the lifting and carrying and setting out were done, told her she would see her the day after tomorrow for a painting play date. "Jacq," is all Nadege gives her, that, and a nod while she's closing her door. Once she was back in their apartment, Jacq remembered she had no idea what to do with her daughter for the next forty-eight hours. It made her ears ring a little. The suicides who took to this peculiar afterlife tended to be lay-abouts, avid readers who like to spend their days in borrowed beds. Jacq's situation was different. She didn't know how many hours she and Joy had spent in every nearby public and school library, Jacq putting in double duty alone bringing books and other school supplies back while Nadege babysat. She'd slit her wrists in the picture book section, slashed her throat in the bathroom, hanged herself over multiple stairwell railings. She'd put a shotgun under her chin under a librarian's desk, guzzled down antifreeze in the staff lounge, all to assemble a decent set of books with which Joy could pretend to complete second grade. Jacq had never done particularly well in school, and now she found herself the only teacher in Los Angeles. The little girl wouldn't hear of going back to the library so soon, and Jacq herself could do without empty, dark stacks just yet.

There was the park, which was to say, all of Los Angeles, but it'd be nightfall soon and this vague place got vaguer out of doors and in the dark. Nadege's and Jacq's apartments had power thanks to a shared generator; Joy and Jacq could retire to separate rooms to watch their own televisions and Blu-ray players, but Joy would go through the new movies they'd brought back from MacArthur Park in an evening.

Jacq had managed to salvage some ice cream after all and that would always placate Joy, but she wanted to be judicious how she used it. No need to shoot the big gun too soon.

A familiar voice called Jacq's name from down at street level as full panic was setting in. Jacq about ran to the window. When she threw the sock with the house keys down she pictured jumping out after it, imagined herself crashing to the ground onto her back and catching the keys.

"How is my favorite lady?" Nash's voice was in the apartment before he was. Both Jacq and Joy are ladies, but they also both know which one of them he means. He went straight to the couch once he was through the door and sprawled, nodding at Jacq on the way over. Joy was in his lap in seconds, her hands in his beard.

"I'm fine," Joy says, sing-songing for him after giving Jacq the silent treatment. Nash looked to Jacq like a skinny Santa with a sunburn, all white hair and jolly but no belly. Instead of red pajamas, he favored long preacher suits with too many buttons. The only red on him was his coloring, which put his people somewhere Southern, maybe Louisiana. Freckles and light eyes. But all she really knew about Nash—black, white or Chinese—was that everyone (including him) claimed he was the oldest local. Or oldest local who wasn't crazy.

"What's this?" Nash was patting at his pockets.

"What is it? What is it?"

He made a show of reaching in and fishing out a hand-carved doll on a stick, a ballerina. It was crafted so that pulling or pushing at the bottom of the stick made it dance a little, twirl and bow.

"It's you," Nash said, handing it over by the stick like a lollipop. "I made it."

Jacq wondered if Nash had already known how make such things when he arrived or if he'd practiced and perfected the skill here. She didn't like how quickly Joy discovered how the ballerina could be made to collapse and spring back, collapse and spring back, over and over.

"What do you say?"

"Thank you, Mr. Nash!"

"That's right!" Nash laughed, channeling an off-brand Santa again. "Thank me!" He nodded over the little girl's head, adopting the tone some adults used when they thought they were being particularly successfully at navigating the gaps in a child's attention. "And how are you doing, Jacqueline?"

"Can't complain. Had a good run today."

"I know, I know." He didn't bother to say directly that he'd already been to the intersection. He always made it a point to pick the bones clean.

Nash made a self-conscious face. "Not to be a bother, but you didn't happen to pull today's paper, did you?"

"Just for you." She produced all the dailies, plus the national papers. Just the way he liked it.

"You are so thoughtful, Jacqueline." He bent over to make eye contact with Joy. "I need my lap back, honey. So I can read the paper. Why don't you take that into the other room."

Joy rolled her eyes but slid off him. Between the couch and Joy's room, the ballerina must have fallen and gotten back up thirty times, picking up speed as Joy slammed her door.

Nash watched Joy leave. When she was gone he pulled out a pair of reading glasses and unfolded *The New York Times*. He snapped each page two, three times before actually reading it.

"It's always a pleasure to read the daily paper."

"I need to get back into that."

"I especially like reading the paper and encountering news about my neighbors."

Jacq could see herself standing in her own living room while an old man made himself comfortable on her couch.

Nash leaned over to scan the other papers' front pages and headlines, made a disappointed face. "I guess we'll have to wait until tomorrow to read about today's escapade."

Usually Jacq did this dance with him, but today she can't muster the energy. "Joy needed some things, Nash."

"Yes, yes, poor Joy. You know, people Here have always met their needs by hunting and gathering." He grinned at her over the top of his glasses, already pleased with the coming punchline. "You, you're like a factory farm."

Jacq took a deep breath. "Everybody eats off of what I pull."

Now it was Nash's turn to roll his eyes. "Jacqueline, I have always eaten well." She didn't doubt it. People "disappeared" every day in Los Angeles, with a fair share ending up Here. Coffee and burgers on every block meant the chances of starving back to death were slim.

"I'm careful. They think it's all a publicity stunt."

"A publicity stunt for what?"

Jacq didn't have an answer.

Nash folded up his newspaper. "It's not them I'm worried about."

"We're fine."

"How many times have you crossed over this week? This month? Since you arrived here? You are the best at this I have ever seen—"

"Thanks."

"I'm not done. Your genius for self-annihilation means you have to know better than most that everyone flinches eventually, leaves a corpse behind."

"I wouldn't do that to Joy."

Nash opened his mouth to say something, but before he could get it out, there was a loud noise outside like a screwed-and-chopped sonic boom. A noise that only existed Here. It was the sound of someone crossing over, of the air and atoms of one place being overwritten by another place's air and atoms. Still, Jacq knows what Nash was going to say, heard it as clear as if he'd shouted it at her and had no rejoinder. The fact that Joy was Here at all didn't say much about what she would or wouldn't do.

Jacq wanted to tell Nash exactly how Joy got Here as soon as they'd arrived. He wouldn't let her, said he didn't care how or why anyone crossed over. He'd talk about getting Joy back There now and then, useless talk. Wait until she was older, he said, until she could better understand her situation.

She'd tried to tell Nadege when it seemed to her that the two of them were a thing. A thing approaching real comfort and routine. She'd tried the middle of the night, when she was sure Joy was asleep in her room. She could see Joy on a baby monitor, could see Nadege in the grey light from the screen.

Nadege stopped her before she could get a full sentence out. Put her fingers against her lips to shush her and rubbed like she was smearing something shameful on.

"You need to choose between telling me and having me."

Jacq thought on that and made like she was zipping her mouth shut. Nadege had grinned at that, forced her fingers past Jacq's lips and teeth into her mouth. It was a few days before Jacq understood the other woman had lied to her. That was four, maybe five weeks ago, and it was the last time Nadege had touched her. Nadege kept her end of an unspoken bargain with regards to Joy but had judged Jacq anyway. She hadn't even needed the actual story.

The only person Jacq could have talked all of this through with was Joy, but that conversation wasn't going to happen for years. She wanted to die every time she thought about having it, and then, just like that, she did.

Laura Lucas

NILSCAPE

The railroad crossing signal erupted into a mess of blinking lights as the black-and-white-striped bar dropped across the road just in front of the car. Maytra hit the brake and flinched simultaneously, though the seat belt didn't allow her to move very far, then relaxed as she realized she had a few minutes to wait. The train was a long one, double-stacked with containers from the port. She took a deep breath and took her hands off the steering wheel.

The pavement was still wet from the rain that had fallen just before lunch. Everything was a muted grey: the sky above her, the road below, and the buildings on either side of the tracks cast in damp concrete. The crossing signal's colors blazed like nothing else in view.

Maytra turned to open her purse lying on the passenger seat so she could get a piece of gum. As her perspective shifted, she realized there was another bit of color in sight, on the wall of the building off to her right.

The building was clearly a warehouse of some kind, with small, dirty windows of the type she always thought of as "squinty brutalist." On the corner of the building, close to the ground, someone had sprayed a phrase in Day-Glo orange paint: "We're not there." There were no other markings and no signature. Weird, she thought. Didn't people usually write, "So-and-so was here"? She'd learned to mostly ignore graffiti years ago, passing so many empty buildings on the way back and forth to work every day. Aside from a few gang territory marks her nephew Tyrell had taught her to recognize for safety reasons, she wasn't much of an authority. Tyrell was a police officer, so his experience was a lot more recent than her vague memories from high school of the black-marker scribbles on the stall doors in the girls' toilets.

The end of the train went rushing past: an honest-to-goodness red caboose. She wondered how many of those were still operating as she pulled out the pack of gum and quickly unwrapped a piece. Popping it into her mouth, Maytra put her hands back on the wheel just as the signal's bar slowly raised itself. She pressed the gas and headed across the tracks. A white hatchback went past in the opposite direction, too fast for her to see the driver. She drove two blocks, then turned left at the corner and headed into the energy of downtown traffic. Navigating the streets with a grace born from memory, she arrived at her building and slipped into her parking spot.

As she rode upstairs in the elevator, it creaked and groaned in weirdly bass tones. Her building sure wasn't one of those new luxury condo towers surrounding South Lake Union like unlit birthday candles, she thought. But it was reasonably priced and the best location she could afford. Rents all over the city were rising as fast as the new skyscrapers.

Maytra stepped out on the fourth floor and walked down to the end of the hall, pulling out her keys as she went. She unlocked the door and turned the knob slowly, pressing one foot into the opening. A small face peered up from just beyond her toes. "Hello there," she said to the small grey kitten. "Nobody's running down the hall today, are they? Nope. You're staying right there."

The kitten mewed twice in response, backing away as she slid her foot forward to block its escape route. She stepped onto the rubber mat, closing the door behind her as she slipped off her office shoes and sighed, wiggling her toes a little. The kitten took this as an opening to pounce.

"Hey! No biting, Shirley." Maytra picked up the kitten and cuddled her for a moment. "You know better. Want some dinner?" Shirley

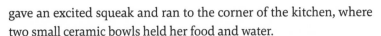

gave an excited squeak and ran to the corner of the kitchen, where two small ceramic bowls held her food and water.

Maytra opened a can of food for the cat, then started making dinner for herself too. By the time her spaghetti was ready, Shirley had stuffed herself with chopped salmon in gravy and retired to a corner of the couch where a small fleece throw had been folded in half. The kitten was curled up on the makeshift bed, issuing tiny snores, when Maytra brought her spaghetti and glass of wine to the table. She ate while watching the local news, muting the commercials. Most of it was rich people complaining about zoning, demanding that the poor folks be shoved down into South Seattle so they didn't block anyone's access to Elliott Bay views.

Later, as she was getting ready for bed, Maytra remembered the graffiti she'd seen on the way home. *We're not there.* Who wasn't? And where *weren't* they? Something about *there* seemed oddly specific.

She climbed into bed and turned out the lamp on her nightstand. Usually she dropped right off, but tonight she lay awake for a while, thinking. *That orange paint color, like traffic cones.* It seemed to glow behind her eyelids.

Eventually, she fell asleep.

The next morning was a holiday. Maytra let herself sleep in a little, just until seven thirty, to mark the occasion. When she started to make breakfast, she realized the egg carton in the refrigerator contained only a single occupant, and the orange juice was perilously low. She left a dish of tuna in cream sauce for the kitten, dressed, and went to the corner store on the next block.

As she was heading back to the apartment, with her triumphant bag of eggs and juice and an extra pack of gum, she saw a red car with its emergency flashers on, sitting in front of a long stretch of concrete retaining wall. The driver, a middle-aged white man whose hair had seen more bountiful days, was talking on a cell phone and looking upset.

Maytra stood back a length or so from the car, but shifted the bag to her right arm and waved her left hand until the driver noticed her. "Need any help?" she called. He shook his head and motioned to the phone, so she nodded and kept walking, circling a bit wide around the car in case the driver opened a door.

Rather than look like she was watching the man in the car, Maytra turned her gaze to the concrete wall. Years ago, some charity group had painted a mural on it with a "message of hope" and a large heart at its center. The message had long since faded out, but the heart was still visible. The neighborhood taggers had apparently taken this as a suggestion, and the wall was covered with declarations of love in every shade Krylon had to offer. Taye & Ruby 4EVR. T-Mac plus Adaiah. Marcell is my man 4 lyfe. Maytra smiled and shook her head at the same time, wondering what sort of qualities a relationship had to have in order to merit being immortalized on the block. Back in her day, you carved your boy's name and yours into a tree, or he did. She wasn't sure which method was less permanent, considering the tiny number of older trees that were left in this city and the wall's odds of being displaced by a glass residential tower within the next few years.

As she came to the far edge of the wall, which curved slightly, she saw one tag that stood out brightly, even against the others, because it was done in Day-Glo orange. "He left us," it read in bleak block writing, the same writing as the tag she'd seen on her way home from work the day before. Again, there was no name. "Us" seemed to suggest a child, though, which would make the anonymous tagger a woman. Maytra was a little surprised. Most of the girls in the neighborhood were happy to see their man put his name (or both of theirs) on a car or abandoned building, but rarely took an interest in doing it themselves.

He left us.

"I'm sorry," she said out loud to the wall, reaching her hand out towards the letters.

She was only a half-inch from touching them when she realized the white man in the car was now watching her, his phone forgotten in his lap. *Crazy black lady*, he was no doubt thinking. She pulled her hand back, quickly faking as though she was just smoothing her twist-out, and turned away, walking faster down the street. She had to force herself not to look back and see if the man was still watching her.

That night, it rained again. Maytra stood at the window in her living room for a long time, looking out at the lights of downtown and the Needle flickering and sparkling in between the heavy rushes of water and wind. Now and then, when things cleared a bit, she could even make out the ferries, far out in the Bay, moving back and forth like flashlights in a blackout.

Shirley didn't like the wind gusts that shuddered around the building, so she was hiding under the couch, only peeping out when the noises grew quiet. The kitten's dinner, beef hearts in thick gravy, sat mostly untouched. Maytra tried to coax her out with a feather-tipped toy, but the big eyes in the darkness under the couch didn't budge. Eventually she gave up and decided to go to bed, leaving Shirley to her own tiny devices.

After putting on her warmest pajamas, Maytra climbed into bed, but left the bedside light on for a bit. She couldn't stop thinking about the words on the concrete wall.

He left us.

James, she thought, and the name hurt all over again. It was years ago now that James had left her, although he hadn't gone voluntarily. She wondered if the same rain was falling on the concrete prison walls around him, and on the cold metal bars. She'd never gone to see him, but she'd also never really dated anyone else after that, either. It was easier to be alone. At least she knew she wasn't going anywhere without herself.

She glanced at the clock on her night table and was surprised to see that it read 12:33. Tomorrow was a workday, so she was going to need some sleep. She turned out the light and put her head down on the pillow. The raindrops clicked and rushed against the window, sometimes sounding like a pebble was being thrown from below against the glass. As if a boy wanted her to open the window, climb out into the night, and disappear into his car, into his arms.

Finally, she slept.

A few days passed, and Maytra felt like there was an itch under the surface of her mind. She went to work, she came home, but underneath, she wondered. She prepared and ate food without really thinking about it, or tasting it. In the center of her mind was a bright spot of orange on grey, like the security lights in a new skyscraper at night, or a tropical sunrise in the middle of rain-soaked downtown.

She waited.

On Friday, a man died.

It happened in Eastlake, on a quiet street with houses fancy by ordinary standards, but barely livable by the city's. The city police were clearing out a group of homeless campers who had set up tents on a vacant slope of land. A few angry words were hurled, but by and large everyone was going quietly. Some already had packed up before the police arrived, and hustled out with what little they had strapped to their backs when the first blue lights appeared.

Maytra only happened to be there because she had an extra-long break for lunch. A meeting had been canceled at work, and she thought it might be fun to go back to a little café with a view of the water that she'd visited once, the year she moved to the city. After turning and searching down street after street, she couldn't find anything that looked like the place she remembered. She was on the verge of giving up as her car rolled past the campsite, and she had a front-row seat when it happened.

The man came out of a tent, and he was on fire.

It was so sudden, so strange, Maytra questioned her own eyes. She blinked a few times, trying to make sure of what she was seeing, as a woman in a ragged old firefighter's coat screamed, and a policewoman ran forward with a blanket, trying to smother the flames. Other people shouted, or ran, but the man himself never made a sound. He stepped out of the tent, a bright star, and then fell forward, and the police-woman threw the dark grey blanket over him and suddenly the light was extinguished. When the blanket was lifted, he never moved. An ambulance came roaring up soon after, full lights and sirens blazing, and took him away. Everyone watched it go, silent and dark, toward the nearest hospital.

Maytra sat in her car for a moment after the ambulance left, then started up and drove herself home. She wrote a brief email to her boss, saying she wouldn't be back that day and to have a good weekend. Then she sat on the couch, turned on the television, and waited.

She didn't wait long.

"Breaking news from the police department," said the usually smiling, blonde local anchorwoman. "A homeless man has died in a suspicious fire at the camp known as the Village. Police aren't sure whether the man died as the result of an accident, or set himself on fire to protest the clearing of the camp today. His identity has not been released, but we'll bring you more on this story as it develops."

Maytra took a deep breath and pressed the palms of her hands together for a moment.

In her mind, she saw the man over and over again, star-bright and then gone.

By Saturday, a candlelight vigil had been planned for that evening to mark the memory of the still-unknown man. Maytra called her nephew, who had her spare key, and asked him to look in on Shirley that evening. "You goin' out?" Tyrell said with a smile in his voice. "Bout time you got yourself a man, Auntie May."

"I'm going to the memorial for that man from the homeless camp," she replied. "I saw it happen—I just happened to be there, but I think I'd like to say goodbye to that poor soul. So will you check in on Shirley, give her a little food if she needs it?" Tyrell promised he would.

The actual site of the camp was still off-limits, as it was considered a crime scene, but a park two blocks down was selected as a suitable place of remembrance. At seven o'clock, Maytra was there with a good-sized crowd, holding a paper-rimmed candle and waiting for the organizers to finish setting up the PA system. The night air was chilly. She buttoned her jacket up underneath her chin, shivering. In the meantime, someone lit their candle, and slowly others touched their wicks to the flame, light spreading one pinpoint at a time across the group. The corner of the park where they had gathered was fairly dark, as it was far from the streetlights. On one side, a row of tall old lilacs was just starting to bloom, their purple smell haloing the crowd. Just behind everyone was the smooth wall of a racquetball court, and as the candlelight brightened, Maytra realized what was on it.

In the center of the racquetball wall, life-sized, was a man made entirely of orange flames, arms raised, just as the man at the homeless camp had stood when he emerged from his tent. Around him were silhouettes of other people in different colors—black, white, blue, brown, red—captured from the waist up, so that their shoulders and heads were visible, though there was no detail on their faces. Above the figure, large block letters in black and white with a single line of orange along their left sides spelled RESTIN PIECE in two tall, vertical columns.

With a shriek of feedback, the microphone turned on, breaking Maytra's reverie. "Good evening, everyone," said a tall Latino man dressed in a plaid shirt and blue jeans. "We're here tonight to say goodbye to a man that none of us knew—in fact, we don't even know his name. What we do know is that he died a terrible death. We don't know if that was accidental, or if he chose that death for himself, but we do know that he was someone. He was someone's child, someone's friend, maybe someone's parent or husband. We know someone, somewhere will miss this man, and mourn him, and we are here to represent them, and to make sure he's remembered."

The tall man paused. "Does everyone have their candles lit?" There were nods and murmurs of affirmation from the crowd.

Why doesn't he say something about the mural? Maytra wondered. It had obviously been made for the memorial.

"If you could all hold your candles with both hands and bow your heads, we're going to have a moment of silence for our friend," said the tall man, lowering his head and taking hold of a candle someone handed him. Everyone lowered their heads, and silence hung over the gathering like a fog. The light from each candle danced and wavered on the face of its holder, and lit up the mural with swirling shadow light, as though the flames on the man in the mural were moving. Maytra couldn't look away from it, though she felt guilty about not bowing her head.

"Thank you," the man said into the microphone, and everyone raised their faces slowly. "I know some of you have flowers and notes and some other remembrances, and we've got permission from the city to put them under and around that tree." He pointed at a tall tree to the right of the racquetball wall. "If everyone could just line up and move over there, we can get everything set, and then we'll take another moment once we have those in place."

The gathered people all began to shuffle slowly in the direction of the tree, trying not to jostle one another—all except for Maytra. She stepped forward, her eyes filled with the mural, the figure afire, the others surrounding it. As she stepped closer, she realized the two columns of text had been colored deliberately, with the black and white letters stacked onto each other to look like tall buildings, and the orange lines marking the glow of windows. She also noticed the curves of the other silhouettes, and how their heads blended into the shoulder lines, giving them a strong resemblance to a group of tombstones. Her hand was slowly lifting up of its own free will, reaching closer and closer to the mural, only a breath away from touching it.

"Ma'am, are you all right?"

Maytra turned her head. A dark-haired young woman with gleaming silver rings in her lip and nose was looking at her with an expression of concern.

"I'm fine, thank you. I just wanted to get a closer look at this."

"At what?" The expression on the young woman's face deepened. "The wall?"

"Well, not just the wall. The mural. I can't stop thinking about that poor man." Maytra's eyes slid back to the orange-hued figure at the center.

"*What* mural?"

The woman's voice had gone up slightly in pitch. Maytra stared at her, thinking it was an odd occasion for a joke, but she seemed serious. "This one right here," Maytra said, pointing at the wall. "Someone went to a lot of trouble to get it up this fast."

The young woman stared at the wall, then back to Maytra, then at the wall again.

"But there's nothing *there*," she said with a slight catch in her voice.

"Are you telling me you can't see that big-ass spray-paint mural covering this wall?"

POC United

Maytra didn't like to swear, but she was beginning to lose her temper. The young woman backed away slowly, her lip trembling. "Sorry, no," she said breathlessly, and then turned and fled into the crowd. Someone yelped that she had stepped on their foot.

Maytra looked back at the mural. It was there, big and clear as a spring day, as her mother used to say. And yet, no one else in the crowd had mentioned it, or even seemed to notice it at all. Could that really be because she was the only one who could see it?

She took a closer look, letting her eyes wander around the edges of the piece. There should be a name on it somewhere, a tag. If there was, however, she couldn't find it. Carefully, she reached up her left hand and touched the mural. She could feel the cold of the concrete wall, so at least that much was real.

She was now standing on the far left end of the wall, and she noticed that along its edge, just visible from where she was, was another set of orange letters.

W
H
E
R
E

These were in the same block print that she had seen twice before, the graffiti left by the still-unknown woman. This time, however, there was one more thing. Below the final E, in the same orange paint, the outline of a right hand had been sprayed, fingers spread. Maytra put her right hand up, spread the fingers out, and laid it over the outlined hand on the wall.

"Listen, I think this lady needs some help," said the young woman with the silver rings. "She was talking about a picture or something that wasn't there. On the wall."

The police officer looked around. "Do you still see her here? What's she look like?"

"Um, a middle-aged lady with, like, black hair in these little spiral curls. She had on a blue sweater, maybe jeans?" She looked around. "I don't see her anywhere."

"And she was looking at something on the wall?"

"Well, that's what she *said*. But there's nothing there—" The woman pointed to the wall and blinked hard, twice.

"Something wrong?" said the policeman.

"No, I just—for a second—there was this orange glow, like a camera flash. I guess someone took a picture." She lifted a hand and brushed her dark hair out of her eyes.

"I don't see her now."

"Well, I can keep an eye out. Maybe she'll turn up." The officer reached into his pocket and pulled out a phone, typing a note rapidly.

"Thanks," the young woman said. She looked around one more time. "I really hope she just went home and made it there safe."

Vickie Vértiz

WINNING PRIZES FOR JUST LIVING

Spring break in LA is one long day at Magic Mountain. My friend
Moses parks his 1985 Caprice Classic next to our chain-link gate. The
engine clicks off and the Led Zeppelin guitar goes quiet. He brought
Eva, Rudy, and my boyfriend Beto to pick me up. We'll be on roller
coasters if only we can get out of the alley I live in. From the family
bedroom, I hear all four doors close. Rudy jokes with Amá. She's
letting them into our cement yard. Then, no more laughing. I can't
hear what they're saying, but I trust they're talking shit—I just don't
know that I'm one of the subjects.

I grab my jacket and go outside as soon as I can, but not fast
enough. Amá is standing in her apron facing her wall of pink gera-
niums. That's when she thanks them for being my friends, especially
after "that thing that happened."

"What thing?" my boyfriend asks. Beto pushes up his glasses on
his nose as if it will help him hear better.

Amá is not talking about the boys who groped me during recess
in seventh grade. She doesn't know about the drive-by shooting
on Loveland Street that Claudia and I ran from, so she isn't talking
about that either. But Amá is talking about Claudia, my ex-best
friend/ex-girlfriend. The catcher from the softball team. The girl
whose braid smelled like cookie dough. The one she caught me
kissing.

POC United

"That girl Claudia molested my Chata," Amá announces. I am still inside, but Moses will give me full details later. "I'm so glad you look out for her. Take care of my Chata."

"Sure we will, señora," Moses says. He uses his obedient son voice. He's afraid of Amá, too—her hands are calloused and biceps are used to hammering whatever calls for it. Moses, my floppy-haired homie, he's the senior who taught me how to drive. He's the only one who knows about me making out with Claudia. Eva and Rudy raise their eyebrows at Amá: *Vickie was molested by another teenage girl?* When I get outside, people have already gotten back in the car. I plop down next to Beto, who barely looks at me. Everyone else is quiet. Moses turns up the radio. Five minutes into the car ride, I ask Beto what's wrong.

"You tell me," he says. "What happened with Claudia?"

I whisper. "What do you mean?"

"Your mom said Claudia molested you."

Cars pass us. I look out and wish I was in one of them, driving the other way. *Chingao, Amá.* I want to pack my one bag and leave home right now. All my business spread around like chisme, and from my own mom. It's not even true.

"She didn't molest me," I say, keeping my voice lower than the music. Eva glances back at us in the rearview mirror. She brushes hair out of her eyes. We drive west. Over the LA River, the water is a trickle. One wall is marked up with tagging in red and blue that says nothing to us. We don't know the language from under bridges; we know distortion on mixtapes. We know boys and girls, not girls and girls. The river is not bursting and dangerous like it was when I kissed Claudia. We made out so hard our lips ached. I don't kiss Beto as hard, but that doesn't mean I don't love him.

We pull up to Eva's house in Bell so she can change clothes. Eva's house is a converted garage that her mom made into a casita. She opens drawers and slams them shut. Her bedroom floor is carpet and it itches my legs. I look anywhere except right at her.

"How could you not tell me you were gay?" Eva huffs. "I've changed in front of you so many times!"

Girl, you are not my type. I think this, but don't say it. We weren't friends last year because she wanted to punch me—for no good reason (something about a guy liking me and not her friend—totally juvenile). I don't say shit. There are only so many times I can take a sucker punch today. I mumble a half-assed, "Sorry," then stare at the photo collages. On her walls are dozens of pictures with Eva in cheer uniforms or with Moses in their matching brown bobs.

Eva's side-eye and pouting follow us into the amusement park. Me and Beto are in five million lines to ride Ninja or whatever shit is cool right now. And next to us, white teenagers are ready to eavesdrop on us.

"I thought I was the only one," he complains.

"I'm sorry," I say. "I should have told you. I didn't know how." There is no shade in this whole park. My skin feels like it's melting off.

I may have to quote that *Sassy* magazine article, the one about how being in love with your best friend is normal. I've repeated that idea to myself for years, but in line right now, I'm empty thought bubbles.

Beto and I wait to ride Colossus, the longest wooden roller coaster in the country. We move inch by inch as the ride creaks and moans around us. People scream in a way I want to but cannot.

I kick into denial, a small flame burning low in my chest. I've only watched one movie to model what I had felt with Claudia. "Maybe we're lesbians," Claudia had said. I wasn't so sure about that—what about all those boys?—so instead we decided that we were bisexuals. This was our coming out: only to each other in the safety of her bedroom. We would not admit this out loud to anyone for years. But this moment, with Beto staring me down, hurt and angry, this is not the time to come out to him. He wants me to tell him that I am his. That I was wrong.

"I should have told you," I say.

"I don't know if I can trust you," he says. I sigh. *It's not that serious. I mean, sure, I lied, but this is only a big deal because Claudia's a girl. He'd be over it if it was some guy I'd slept with.*

The roller coaster carts roll up. Moses and Rudy shoot me weak smiles. Eva is still sour. We board. The train turns hard on the first curve, and I think I've made progress with Beto—his weight is leaning into me. All 180 pounds of him. *It's going to be okay.* Pero no—he scoots away as soon as the next turn comes. This is gravity.

I cling to the cold rails, face the sharp drops. After so many turns, I forget I'm sad and laugh. My belly is in my throat and I laugh harder. Beto's the student body president and I'm his girlfriend, the parliamentarian, a position he handpicked for me when I lost vice president. He is my normal. If not for him, I would have nowhere to go when Amá and Dad fight. Lately their fighting is more vicious: Amá throws oranges at Pop when he comes back from his other vieja's house. Now that is a drive-by I can't avoid. I can't stay in a house like that. I let my weight lean all the way into Beto. *He can take it, I know he can.* The sun is setting, and this will soon get better.

Rudy carries a small box with funnel cake and french fries. The sugar makes Eva lighten up. She takes out her camera and snaps photos of Moses and me at a lunch table. He makes me go get BBQ sauce with him.

"You okay?" he says.

"Sure," I go. "My pinche mom ratted me out. I feel great!"

"Eva will get over it. Rudy doesn't care. These fuckers will forget all about it."

"The thing is," I say, "I'm not sorry I did it. Just that we got caught." I lean on the metal ledge where they keep the condiments.

"Yeah, but people are dumb and won't understand. Maybe you shouldn't brag yet. Your boy's definitely not ready. Look at that fool."

Beto is busying himself by taking several fries off my plate, as usual. I want to yell at him to get his own, but I'm already on his shit list. I smile at him. He catches me watching him and, like a kid who got caught taking money, he smiles back all coy.

"I'm gonna wear this fool down, watch."

"Oh I'm sure you will." Moses hands me a couple of white paper cups with BBQ sauce in them. "Here, carry this. Look alive."

When it gets dark, the cold is not as bad as I thought it'd be. My jacket is enough—what I have is enough: a boyfriend and girl I still love, even though it's not like that. On the drive home I scratch Beto's hair until he falls asleep. *No que no?* Putty in my hands.

Moses turns into my alley. His headlights illuminate the wall at the far end, a tall soundwall no one's bothered to cover in ivy. There's a message scrawled on it in crooked red spray paint:

"Fuck Vicky."

We get out of the car to inspect. The marks are unsure and childlike.

"What the fuck, man," I say.

"Stupid fuckers can't even spell your name right," my friend Rudy says.

Whoever wrote it clearly used spray paint for the first time. This is not the handiwork of world-famous tagger Chaka. Whoever told me to fuck off has clearly written it with their feet.

"And I thought people hated me the most!" Eva laughs. "You win." We all laugh loud, relieved something else is wrong now. Somebody else but me is fucked up.

"It has to be Pánfila," I say. Rudy shakes his head no.

Pánfila, my old best friend with thick legs, is on a school-wide campaign talking shit about me: at the school newspaper, with the yearbook kids, and in the student body room to anyone who'll listen: "Vickie's a bitch. She thinks she's better than everybody. She thinks she's all that. "

Pánfila hates me because a boy she likes has a crush on me—I may be fanning that flame a little, but fuck her, right? I steal glances and joke with him, but is it my fault dudes like shit like that? Pánfila's so mad she even made up a new class favorite category for me: Biggest Ego.

"Dude, don't even defend Pánfila," I tell Rudy. "You know she's crazy."

As additional revenge, Pánfila tried getting Rudy to sleep with her. She told him: "My braces make my blow jobs feel hotter." Poor Pánfila—no one would want to put themselves in a mouth full of metal.

Eva and I exchange looks, like, *Maybe you deserve it, Vick.* I had a crush on Pánfila's boy, it's true, except mine was really, really tiny. Probably because it was some kind of power trip. You know, a "who can get him first" kind of thing. Guess I didn't stop soon enough.

"Don't feel bad, Vick. That's the shittiest tagging ever," Moses says. "I bet she paid them in blow jobs."

We all laugh except for Rudy, the only one who knows for sure.

"Call me tomorrow?" I ask Beto. He nods and gives me a little peck. I take it. I take it because I am not giving up all of this just to correct my mom and tell her what I really think: that I'd sleep with Claudia again, and, with any luck, maybe I will again someday.

Amá has pinto beans on the stove when I walk into the house. They make the house steam and shrink. Pop is asleep on the couch.

"How was it, Chata?" She is in a great mood, smiling at my homecoming instead of railing about how I'm a pata de perro, out on the street instead of home.

I tell Amá I had fun and get ready for bed. My little brothers are asleep. I pretend she's done nothing wrong. Amá can think I'm a victim because her baby can't be anything but perfectly straight. But her Catholic Chicana baby is definitely gay, okay. She loves that I currently appear straight, with straight friends, and am going to college in the fall. Maybe she is a great actor too. We are both amazing actors, winning prizes for just living.

My eyes close, knowing the crooked graffiti will get painted over by the city tomorrow. Of course, the words will still be underneath.

They still are.

Natalie Graham

UNBURNING THE BODY

for F. M.

Begin with failing
at words, amnesia in your mouth,
menthol opening you,
fresh cigarettes.

Taste peppermint, salt,
a wet, third thing,
a spectacular alloy,
electrum.

Carry the charge up
the spine or through a channel
worn smooth.
A clipped broadcast
feeds noise.

You muddy
the message.
Try this:

Enter through the slit.
Lick the color of teeth,
Lick, lightening a scowl,
Lick, loosening a cloud.

Graffiti

This is the break
from the daily fouling,
its hard crunch,
its sickening heavy,
its throttle,
its fallowing singe.

This body, a map on top of a map,
fights its folds and spread.
We come real soon.

Simmer, stretch and burnish.
Burnish a crumpled shadow.
Coil and split.
Split, the wants from worry.

Tuck into this shade.
Lean home.
Hold.
Hold or disappear.

Pallavi Dhawan

STRANDED

I am mentoring a nineteen-year-old college student. She is Egyptian, tall with pale skin, square glasses, and a smile pasted on her face. Sometimes the glasses slip down her nose and I want to reach out and push them back. I feel protective. She reminds me of myself at nineteen. Only she doesn't need my protection. She hugs with all the strength in her sturdy frame, and she stands firm and fixed on her feet, an extraordinary feat for any young brown girl.

She needs to interview me for her internship. She is still bright and doe-eyed, her face softly crumpling into light laughter. I take her to my favorite artisanal bread factory for lunch. When we enter, she forges ahead of me, stomping sure-footedly in black leather boots, her square heel gathering the loose grains and flour that dust the ground. Between mouthfuls, she tells me she is interested in a legal career, but her parents want her to pursue medicine. She enrolled in biology during her first term and sat dutifully through the class, struggling to follow the material with interest. After barely passing, she argued with her parents over her major. She is still hoping to persuade them that her decision to switch to a liberal arts degree is not the major transgression her parents must speak of only in whispers, or else not at all.

I give her credit for trying. When I applied to college, I listed my major as biochemistry; during orientation, I only signed up for general education classes like anthropology and literature. I changed my major soon after to political science and told my mother in the kitchen as she washed the dishes. She let her hands drop into the suds and managed to steady her rage until she finished the washing, though her eyes twitched with the effort. She dried her hands on the kitchen towel and told me I was ruining my life. I stood for a few moments, fighting the urge to run. My childhood instinct, built on regular blows, was to hide or flee, even in the absence of real danger. I stood still and repeated that I had made up my mind. She did not raise her hand. She just left the room. But my face flushed red, as if she had struck me.

I heard her asking my father what I was thinking, how I acted like I knew everything.

"She is a child, she knows nothing."

I *was* a child once, with a different name. I was born Sonali. Then, during the summer after second grade, I went to India to visit my mother's family for the first time. Before meeting aunts and uncles and cousins, I had to greet the country. She first hit me with smog and dust, followed by stifling heat and humidity that dissolved me like magic. She turned the clock back to the time of my birth date. Further, to the birth of my ancestors, further still, to the time of the stars that dot the heavens—and the pundit, looking heavenward, read my fortune in a small shack, my mother and I seated at his feet.

"Change her name," he advised my mother, "to one starting with the letter P or J. If she remains Sonali, her life will be marred by sorrow." What mother would want that? Two months after landing in India, I returned to California as Pallavi.

I had to begin again as the girl with the new name, the name that no one could pronounce. On this name, tongues tripped and laughed and skittered away, afraid to reach into the fog that draped around me like a veil of sorrow. So I reached out and handed it over. Take it. Make it yours. And they did. They took Pallavi and renamed it Pellavi, and then, Pellavi became Pellvi, and that was my name from eight to eighteen. I let them do it. I helped when they struggled, correcting their mispronunciations by substituting my own. The meanest ones sharpened their tongues on it and spit it back at me, mocking and cruel. In that time, I grew crocodile skin, clandestine shadow skin that prickled. My body still remembers. I align my back with walls, slithering lizard-like, camouflaging, disappearing before I can draw blood. *It is for your own protection. Don't touch. Don't even look.* Before I can turn, you are gone.

Sometimes, I dream of Sonali. She is a girl who loves to wander in white through strawberry fields, leaning over to pick the succulent red drops, her skin stained pink. She opens up her face to the sun and inhales the honeyed air. She crunches her teeth on rainbow lollipops and falls in love with everyone she meets.

If I lived in India, concerned relatives would be asking after me, prodding my mother. *Have you started looking? She is not getting any younger.* My mother married my father at twenty-four. She did not worry that she hardly knew him. She made the most practical decision at the time. She is of the mind that life can be distilled to a series of boxes on a checklist. I have checked off very few.

I had my first kiss at nineteen. He was Indian, though he had never lived in or even visited India. He spoke a jumbled patois of English and Bajan and my name in his mouth was soft. He was a bartender, a sailor hardened on the beach like the colored pebbles that appear after seawater churns broken glass. The wave in his hair and the calluses on his skin told the story of a life lived in perpetual motion through wind and water, unhindered but for the drag of waves on the hull of his boat. When he said it was not realistic to carry on a relationship because of the distance—he lived in Barbados, I in Carlsbad—I cried into the phone and told him I would never meet anyone like him again. He was a mature twenty-two (experienced in all the ways Indian parents dread), and he replied practically, trying his best to soothe me, "You will kiss many more men after me. You won't remember me." He was right as to the first part but otherwise wholly wrong. Now, I suspect he understood that he was lying to me, but I am grateful he did, because I might have thrown myself off the cliff and swum to Barbados if it meant I could taste the salt on his skin. I imagine the sea air in the Caribbean tastes different than the air in Carlsbad, imbued with the sweat of indentured Indian servants brought by British ships to farm sugarcane fields, their fragrant breaths seeping into the sugar. *You can force us out of India, but...*

What does a girl know of her own body at nineteen? I knew nothing then, only that I didn't like the sheen of the sun on my skin for it made it browner and crisper, frightening to me like charred meat sticking to bone. My body still scares me for what it holds inside, for what it is unwilling to grant, for how it refuses to bend or yield, even to me. I push people away. I see danger in longing and I avoid it diligently, refusing to make eye contact, staring instead at the glittering asphalt, the "I love you's" and "I was here's" carved inside the broken sidewalk, taunting me. *I was not here. I am nowhere.*

Nineteen-year-old me takes it all for granted. The softness and suppleness of her skin, the curl in her hair, the glint in her speckled brown-green eyes, not yet tired from all they have to bear witness to. Her life hasn't even started. I imagine I can see her stars aligned in the sky and I play the pundit.

"Stay focused. Don't let others tell you how to live your life."

We tear into our loaves and I am keenly aware of how my mouth moves when I chew, how the flour coats the ends of my lips. I am aware of my mouth in the way of one not lately kissed.

Somehow I pulled myself up, I tell nineteen-year-old me, despite my parents. Now that my parents have stopped telling me how to live, I wonder if they have written me off. "Focus on your personal life" is advice I haven't heard in a long time, words I yearn for as the glow of the moon inscribes a hollow into the night sky. At the end of every conversation, my mom used to ask: "Aur kuch? Anything else?" Her words, lilting, would rise, stretching up toward the desired answer, before dropping at my actual response and resolving in a final staccato goodbye. She has stopped asking even that question, though I will ask myself sometimes, *What else is there? Is there anything else?* I do not know, but I listen for the answer in the music that moves between the branches and my bones, sometimes sounding like a dirge, at other times, like hope.

L. Penelope

LOOP

I wear an oversized hoodie so he won't know whether there's still a baby in me. I'm not sure which outcome he's hoping for.

The house is not what I expect. It isn't in a bad neighborhood. There are no signs out front, no line of shivering junkies stretching out the door, clamoring to get in. No crack vials or used needles litter the ground. Pink hydrangeas and some plant with a firework of electric-blue flowers frame the front porch. It looks like just another house on another street in Any City, USA. Then again, this is the first rehab clinic I've ever been to. Maybe they all look like this, hidden behind a wall of topiary perfection. Hope in bloom.

Heat pools in the center of my chest, giving way to a chilling sort of emptiness. I turn around a dozen times, but can't bring myself to leave. Early morning birdcalls trill. I haven't seen this side of 7 AM—the side when you've just gotten out of bed, instead of having just gotten into it—in a long, long time.

There is still time to turn back, not go through with this. Avoid the whole thing. Still time.

Until the door opens and Danny walks out onto the porch. He wears a black t-shirt and sweatpants, and, in any other house on the street, I'd think he'd be heading out for a morning run. Both our clothes conceal truths we'll have to stop hiding from. I stuff my hands in my pockets, pushing away thoughts of how his skin feels under my fingertips.

He looks at me expectantly.

"Your hair," I say. "It's so curly. I never knew."

Loose, soft-looking black curls envelop his head. He reaches up as if to run his hand through it, but stops mid-motion and drops his arm back to his side.

"It hasn't been this long in forever." A tentative smile teases his lips; the rest of his face remains a mask.

He takes a single step forward, stopping at the edge of the porch. Standing on the sidewalk, I'm at eye level with his sneakers. One of his shoelaces has almost worked its way out of its knot. I wonder how long he has been awake, or if this is a result of some new carelessness that has emerged through mental clarity. We regard one another through new eyes. His hair is not the only thing that has changed.

"So," he says. I wait for more, but it doesn't come.

"So," I finally say, wishing I knew what came next.

What came first was the summer we met. He was thinner then, with a dusting of closely cropped hair prickling his scalp. He cut it himself, using an ancient pair of clippers some old housemate had left behind.

There was a mirror bolted to the door of the hall closet, and he'd stand there buzzing off his hair in the middle of the hallway— always managing to get the back perfect. With the door open, the hall mirror would catch the reflection of the one mounted above the bathroom sink.

"The bathroom, that's where people usually do things like shave their heads," I'd chide. But he'd shush me and apply his finely honed focus to the task at hand, removing the unwanted new growth in even rows—back to front— traversing the whole, beautiful globe of his head, twice.

Watching the ritual was calming, watching him do just about anything seemed to quiet the dizzying pace of my mind. His motions were so deliberate and purposeful. Slow and even. Nothing to tip me off. I was the one whose limbs jittered like I was craving a fix—always in motion. Though the only thing I was addicted to was him.

That first summer I'd follow him around. Watch him fold laundry, dry dishes, cook eggs. Admire how much clarity and attention he paid to these tasks. His concentration was currency. Watching him glide the steel wool across the grate of the grill top might have been what made me fall in love with him. Then again, I'm pretty sure I was destined to love him.

Of course, he was seeing someone else when I first met him. Someone boring and narcissistic, the way all his girlfriends had been. But I was undaunted. My efforts were like a steady drip on a stone until his girlfriend dumped him in July after finding a pair of panties under his bed.

Ninety days ago, I walked away from Danny and into a fog. Actually, he walked away from me, rubbing his wrists where the handcuffs had chafed. No contact. Those were the rules. No calls. No email. No texts. I would have even considered writing him a letter—by hand—but those weren't permitted either.

The last words he said to me were, "Whatever you decide, I'll understand." The doors clanked and it was me alone in the world for three months. Well, alone if you don't count the five-week-old baby growing inside me.

Whatever I decide. Like whether he'd still be a father when he got clean.

When I was six, my father showed up at school one day and pulled me out, claiming I had a doctor's appointment. I'd been a notoriously healthy child, the strength of my constitution repelling colds and flu; even the chicken pox escaped me as it claimed most of my classmates, so it should have been a red flag.

I was excited to be getting out of school and to be spending time with my dad. At the time, I thought of him as a big man, huge like a wrestler with rippling muscles and a booming voice. But in reality, he was of average height and build. Average in just about every way.

We drove out of the sun-speckled, tree-lined streets of our neighborhood and to a much nicer one, with huge houses that looked like castles, set back on expansive yards, much larger than even the fields at school.

We pulled into a circular driveway in front of a sparkling white mansion that could have housed royalty. A maid opened the door and ushered us into a high-ceilinged room filled with gleaming objects. Everything made my eyes hurt.

A sheen of sweat covered my father's face and his fingers danced in the air. They moved like they were poised on top of piano keys, instead of hanging at his sides, hovering next to his thighs. His eyes were glazed over, shining and glassy like everything else there. He didn't look at me as he left the room, telling me to sit quietly and be sure not to touch anything. After he had been gone for what seemed like hours to my overwhelmed mind, a different door opened and another man came into the room. I had been waging a war inside myself to follow my father's instructions and sit quietly. My instinct was to run up to every beautiful, glistening thing I saw and explore it. Feel it under my skin and cover it with tiny, smudged palm prints. But I pushed those feelings back, determined to be good.

That was the last time I remember trying.

The man smelled of mint. He sat across from me and asked if he could take my picture. I nodded and smiled automatically when he produced the camera. He told me this wasn't the smiling kind of picture, and that I should look at the camera as if it were a slice of my favorite cake and I was dying to have it.

"Look at it like your mouth is watering," he said. "Have you ever felt like that?"

I nodded again—my voice unable to appear for this man. Another rarity.

He got up and sat down next to me, his large knees brushing my leg. A long finger brushed my bangs back from my forehead.

"Let's get a close-up," he said.

He held the camera inches from my face and asked me to pout my lips like I was blowing a kiss. Mint filled my nostrils.

On his way out the door he paused, saying, "See you again soon, sweetheart."

My father returned shortly, patted me on my shoulder and we went home. We spent the rest of the afternoon watching TV together. Not the kids' shows I usually watched, but grown-up shows about cops and robbers and judges.

He told me not to tell Mom about the man with the camera. That it had to be our secret, or something very bad would happen to him. But I burst into tears the night before the school pictures, seized with an uncontrollable fear. My mother asked me questions over and over, very slowly, and I knew I'd done something wrong. Her whole body vibrated with suppressed rage, her face so taut I thought it would crack, but instead of yelling at me or giving me a spanking, she just held me close to her for a long time.

That weekend, Mom and I moved into my grandmother's house and it was a long time before I saw my father again.

Danny regards me through long black lashes that always made me want to sigh. His face seems more solid somehow, like all that time before he'd been in flux or I'd been looking at him through a filter. That gauzy, diffused light is gone and here we are standing across from one another, the post-dawn light slicing our faces.

"What did you decide about the baby, Reza?" His jaw is tight.

"Let me ask you this," I respond. "What do you think it's like having a junkie for a father?"

He breaks off eye contact with me, looking down the street. "You tell me. I only know what it's like to have a bastard for a father."

The last time I saw my father, he was limping across a street downtown, dragging one of his legs behind him like some kind of injured animal. Stains patterned his clothing. He shouted at a turning vehicle that nearly clipped him in the crosswalk, and I could see not much was left of his teeth. He passed right by without recognizing me. Didn't ask me for money either. I hadn't known whether he was still alive or not, and in that moment, I still wasn't sure.

But he wasn't my biggest betrayal.

I'd never seen my father hovering at the edge of consciousness on the floor, half under the couch, his breaths so slow and shallow I'd had to put a mirror up to his nose to see whether they were coming at all. I'd never cried in an ambulance, in a hospital room, in a courtroom as he was given the choice of jail or rehab for the discovery of a stash deemed too large for personal use only.

My father kept all that away from me. Placing me instead on a brightly lit stage, exposed and ready for my close-up. After that, I sought out the flash of the bulbs, the press of bodies, the noise of crowds, the shiny bottles. Moving, always moving, just fast enough to show up as a blur.

My eyelids were encrusted with pink glitter the first night we met. My hair was wild, deodorant had long since failed, and my voice was going hoarse from screaming during the bands that had performed after us. Our show had been amazing, and I was caught up in the post-performance high, thrumming even more than usual with aimless energy looking for a receptacle.

Danny stood off to the side, arms folded, looking serious—appearing much too thin and wiry to be working security for a club, and all the more dangerous because of it. In my mind, he was one of those British soldiers in front of Buckingham Palace that couldn't smile or react at all no matter the taunt. I teetered over, unsteady on my four-inch heels, and flirted viciously. I asked him how he liked the show. If he'd been impressed by my vocal prowess. I offered him a quickie in the green room if he'd leave his post.

He regarded me coolly, maintaining his vigilance over the crowd behind me. I wobbled, losing my balance, and his arms shot out to steady me, grabbing my waist. He righted me, then plucked the drink from my hand and set it down.

"You have a lot of stage presence," he said, releasing his other hand from my waist. "But you need to work on controlling your voice." His hands were so steady.

I wrap my arms around myself, wishing for something familiar to hold onto. This new Danny, whose shoelace has almost completely worked itself loose, is a stranger.

He exhales and sits down on the step like the only thing that has been keeping him upright was the air in his lungs. Resting his elbows on his knees, he turns a purple rubber bracelet around and around on his wrist. I can't read the writing on it, but I guess it has something to do with his sobriety. He looks at me with the old intensity. It startles me because, for the past few months, I haven't been sure what was real and what wasn't. What had been him and what had been the drugs. I'm relieved to see that what I thought of as his soul remains.

He releases another pent-up breath and drops his hands. His eyes leave my face and I feel lost. Weightless. Floating in space, waiting for some passing debris to smash into me.

Then he looks down and notices that his shoelace has come loose. His sneaker sits half untied, the lace dangling in the air.

The first finger and thumb of his left hand grab it and pull, releasing the knot completely. His other hand comes down and grabs the other lace. He discovers that the two sides are uneven, so he loosens all the laces, pulling them through the lace holes starting nearest his ankle and moving out to the toe. Then he pulls each section of lace taut, applying equal pressure to either side. When he gets to the end, the loose strings are perfectly even, and he ties them deftly into a perfect, symmetrical, crisp bow.

When his hands stop moving, I discover that I have been holding my breath. I inhale deeply and unzip my hoodie.

The panties his girlfriend found weren't mine, as it turned out. One of his roommates had hooked up in his room the week before, while he was at work. After the girlfriend left, he called me. I showed up on his doorstep with a six-pack. We sat on the stoop making quick work of it.

Lying in bed that first night, with only moonlight to guide me, I traced the old scars crisscrossing his body. Cigarette burns and longer, deeper gashes formed a pattern. They were like graffiti tagged on his skin—his father: not a monster, but an artist. He stroked my own smooth, unmarred skin, and I wished for a moment that my scars were on the outside.

My father had taken me to see the man with the camera twice more before my mother found out. Something I'd tell Danny about months later, lying in bed like this, trading war stories. But that first night, the unwelcome memory made me shiver. I drew his heavy arm around me to lock me in place by his side. The rise and fall of his chest was the drumbeat, anchoring the melody of the night. A tune began forming on my lips and I fell asleep humming the refrain.

Tongo Eisen-Martin

CUT A HAND
FROM A HAND

"if you reverse the car any farther,
you will run over all the scenes in the back of your mind"

I never cared for teachers...just the pattern of fainting spells
     induced by wall art.
Propaganda is courage, man

The price sticker hid my tattoo
—I treasure my problem with the world

"My mother becomes from Brooklyn first thing in the morning"
—a proverb around these parts
          proverb or peasant entrance password

Writing short notes to famous Europeans
On the backs of post cards
With ransom requests

They reply with a newsreel or cigarette announcement (I can't tell
     the difference)

                              —Noble dollars then you die inside
                                        (but only inside)

"They call it, 'sleeping deeper than your stalker.'
And stalker is all that badge makes you,"
says a great spirit dressed in the bloody rags tuxedos became

meanwhile my punch is feared by no one
"Proud of yourself?" I ask the fret hand

"Porch Lights" is what they call our guns
I've seen this house in a dream
I've seen this chair on behalf of a dream

I believe a trumpet was the first possessed object to fly

"keep going," she cheers

the draft in the room becomes a toddler
obsessed with the altar
the altar becomes a runaway train
got a thousand paintings cascading down my skinny arms
Dictionaries piling up to the window bars

basements called dope-fiend cocoons
crowd into the part of my mind
referred to as my heart
—a reminder to the population that
your blanket can work with
or against you—

human reef/
we will be a big human reef
for concepts that finally gain a metaphysical nature
and they will swim around our beautiful poses

we stop being flashbacks
then stop being three different people
then I was alone [the pistol is one city away]

one of the drug triangle's lines runs through my head

Tongo Eisen-Martin

tap the bottle twice and consider the dead refreshed
"don't you want to rest your bravery?
don't you want to be a coward for a little bit?"
—back and forth to a panic attack with no problems nor fears

a man gets a facial expression finally
a Friday finally goes his way
his life is finally talked about happily in his head

> *I can't possess the body of a hermit*
> *I must be the last of his smoke*
> *Now running away with three blocks of alley*
> *Tucked under my arm*
> *You ever see a man*
> *get to the bottom of his soul*
> *in a car ride down a missing cousin's street?*
> *half step to the right*
> *I mean I took the whole car outside of history*
> *Half step to the right*
> *I mean a whole pack of wolves stepped to my left*
> *—Deep in the recesses of the main recess*

"road marker" is what I called the light bulb we had for a sun
a whole civilization might slink to the sink
chain gang shuffling next to a sucker

—the long look in the mirror [a stack of money starts talking from
four cities away]

Tongo Eisen-Martin

MAY WE ALL REFUSE TO DIE AT THE SAME TIME

"I believe I wasn't born yet, when a young woman put her first gun
        under a car seat,"
The painter explained
in front of his work
with a .38 in his back pocket

Combination of conversations you may call it:
The day all the saints clocked in late
mixed with the first serious talk
seven-year-old best friends have about war.

What war stories taught me I now teach you

"the world is just a constellation of walls.
Twitch a little less than everyone else.
That's the key."

I miss her
Or is the cage of a westbound interstate bus ride beautiful when all
        but three people are asleep

I'm writing poems for the rest of my life again

Taught by the greats:
>"friends make friends. You just be a good liar."
>"you would not believe the grains of blue
>I found after they laid me to ground."
>"fit in, youngster."
>"fit in, trigger man."
>"watch your nickname mean something to more than five
>people."

the newspaper is on fire. forget about the car.

A white giant was born without a third dimension.
It wanders under county jail slippers and people who smoke by
themselves in old city parks

Gas chambers are not complicated
Have a drink. Go to work.

"They lynched his car too. Strung it up right next to him... You see, a
smart man makes up his own set of holidays... Mind. I had a mind
once. Served my immediate family well. But that's all over now.
Now I live in america... A smart man switches the dates around of
his holidays too. Because enemies have a sense of humor."

A most impressive reimagining of a painter

Up here
Where the tenth floor
Might as well be a cloud of dust
Or a version of myself that
I can point your attention to
While I count my money and curse mankind

The best way to pay me
Is in my left hand
While my right is juggling

A cigarette
A steering wheel
And a negotiation with the ruling class

Maybe you are not a sleepy employee in a project lobby
Maybe you are blood on a fiber
Maybe you are my friend

I have ruled the world.
Let me sleep this off.
Is that your tongue in the sky?
That's the only weather I need.

Lazy conversation
—the only way physics advances

my right hand jogs away from the band

this getaway is live

this instrument
is not yet invented

Coming down
With the rest of the sound
—the young woman and me about to be born

"And there. There is you. Dancing with someone's daughter in front
of the precinct"

Tongo Eisen-Martin

CHANNELS TO FALL ASLEEP TO

While shoe box to shoe box travels my childhood

Professionals roll garbage cans around a conference room
Half the size of a holding tank
Half the hope of a holding tank
Full of third world retail flattery
"nothing wrong with the blind leading the blind,"
                              we think they just said

                    the entire train station crouches behind a piano player
                         and why should Harlem not kill for its musicians
                                              "He is in a dream"
                                              "A spirit world"
                                      "I should introduce myself"
                                      "And convince him to sleep"

porcelain epoch
succeeding for the most part
dying for the most part
married for the most part to its death

when a hostage has a hostage
that is u.s. education

Graffiti

stores detach their heads
and expect you to do the same when you enter

God says, "do not trust me in this room"

Two fascists walk into a bar
One says, "let's make a baby."
The other says, "let's make three... and let the first one eat the
    other two."

your sky or mine
read from
the book of pool room enemies

"I'm the best kind of square. Poor and in love with the 1960s. The
first picture I ever saw in my life faded from my storytelling a
long time ago."

Not even ten years old
And most of you are on my shoulders

The store's detached head smiled

casually be poor
    teach yourself
    how to get out of this room
    and we'll leave you enough blood
    to turn off the lights
    on your way out

casually be poor
    they are all cops when you are poor

Lin Y. Leong

THE GIRL AND THE MOTH

It was said of the first moths made for the Emperor's purpose that they were fashioned of paper, itself made from the thickly furred leaves of the wild purple sage plant. That was what gave their wings their velvety toughness, the hint of green and silver and purple, iridescent, as they rocked at rest, waiting for their subjects to understand their fates. That was what gave them their fragrance.

It was this fragrance—perfumed green, pungently bitter and sweet—that had announced to her she was no longer alone in her little cavern. The smell of the place did not change much from day to day—damp earth smelled ever of damp earth, and even more so when rain approached—and she had been too sick to seek out the sun to try to dry out her bones to keep them from aching so. When she woke from her latest sleep, she had thought at first she had wandered out in her slumber to lie amongst the herb fields of the nearest farm. Suicidal, but perhaps her body had finally been called by her sleeping mind to do what her waking mind was too afraid to.

But, no, her body still rested on cold, hard rock. And beneath that strange, sweet fragrance, the scent of damp earth was still full in the air. Slowly, her eyes adjusted from the darkness of dream sleep to the low light in the cavern. And then she saw it—one of the Emperor's moths. It was as big as the span of her hand, spread wide. It perched on the rock above her head, wings splayed to show its imperial colours to full effect, its feathery antennae poised to spell out in gold what she had been waiting for these past four years.

Her death orders had come at last.

She lay there, frozen, staring at it. Once her heart had climbed out of her mouth and back down her throat to return to her chest, she rolled out from her sleeping nook as quickly as she dared.

The moth did not move.

Barely taking her gaze from it, she gathered rocks, the worn old basket, and a long stick. One wavering antenna curled the slightest degree in her direction, as if tasting the air.

That mere twitch was already too much for her. In one quick motion, she flicked the moth off the wall to the ground with her stick. It landed with a slight thud, as if a small bird had fallen from the sky. She trapped it with her old asan pod basket. The rocks went over the basket's edges to secure it. And just like that, it was done. She had caught herself one of the Emperor's death moths.

It did not fling itself against the basket, batting its wings furiously for escape, like a bird would do, but lay absolutely still on the ground, as if stunned. Then, it stretched out its shivering wings so that silver iridised to lavender and jade, the mothy equivalent of a yawn. Gold dust drifted from its curling antennae and wings.

She could not help but think it was a trifle smug.

She had been too young to remember much of when the purge began, only that there had been quiet nights of intense whispering between her parents for weeks before the soldiers came to their house. Mama had told her to be good and quiet and to do what she was told, but also to stay out of their way. So she had retreated to the kitchen to sit with Porpor.

The soldiers had brought wheelbarrows with them, and they emptied her house of books and paper and every single writing implement. Even the blue paint Mama had mixed up for her had been taken, along with her brushes and the beginnings of what had been a picture of their house and her family—Mama, Baba, Porpor, and her—all lined up

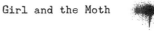

outside, with only half the sky painted on. All was wheeled outside and dumped into the cart waiting on the road. Other soldiers were checking their neighbours' houses and emerging with wheelbarrows full of the same. Mama and Baba stood by the cart horse, talking with one of the soldiers. Baba's gestures were getting bigger, his voice increasing in volume, and Mama had put her hand on his back discreetly in warning.

A soldier had seen her watching them from inside the kitchen. He'd called to her, and Porpor nudged her forward.

The man gave her a smile she did not trust. "Mui-mui. Show me your hands."

She was not his little sister. But she remembered what Mama had said, and so she thrust her hands forward, though she curled her bare toes against the smooth wooden floor to do so.

He took her hands gently in his grip and examined them, turning them over, even looking between her fingers and under her fingernails.

"How old are you, Mui-mui?"

She shook her head and turned to go back to Porpor, but he tightened his grip on her so she could not leave.

"How old is the girl?" the soldier asked Porpor.

"Three. Too young for this business." Porpor nodded toward her hands, caught tight in the soldier's grip, then at the front door, where her father was still on the verge of shouting.

She was five. She had opened her mouth to correct Porpor, but her grandmother shot her a look that made her shut her mouth. "She only plays with paints to make pictures. I am sure you did the same yourself at that age. She knows well enough not to meddle in things beyond her reach."

The soldier smiled. "If only more people had that attitude. None of this would be necessary."

Porpor gave a smile that was not a smile at all and said nothing.

The soldier turned his attention back to her, crouching down so that they were eye to eye. He was a little younger than her father. "You know not to make words with your hands, don't you, Mui-mui?" He squeezed her hands again, not painfully tight, but firmly enough that she could not break from his hold.

She curled her toes beneath her again, uncurled them. A single stroke against the smooth wood with her big toe.

"That's only for the Emperor to do, and the special people he has asked to work for him," he said.

She nodded. Another stroke across with her bare toe.

"Good girl. The magic is not for the likes of you, nor me."

She finished the final stroke with her big toe. *No*, she had written. She began the character again. "The mages," she said.

The soldier smiled. "That's right. Only the mages." He looked behind her at Porpor. "She's a smart one. You might want to watch her." He turned back to her. "The moths will know if you misbehave. They need only to be given your name, and they will find you. No matter where you are, no matter how you try to hide."

They left the city the night the soldiers had raided their house. Porpor stayed behind, too frail to make the journey. Her grandmother had kissed her forehead and eyelids, stroked her hair, and told her to be good. That was the last time she saw Porpor.

They travelled beyond the outskirts of the farms that surrounded the city, all the way until the land turned too marshy for anything to grow but the asan mangroves that edged the coast. There, Baba and Mama built another house. Attached to the front door was a little jade ornament in the shape of a fish, meant for protection and luck.

There was no more talk of magic, no more lessons in writing. Soon after, Mui-mui was born. If Mama and Baba had given her baby sister any other name, they did not tell anyone or use it. And from then on, she was only called Jeh-jeh, Big Sister.

Little sisters could pester. By all that was good and great, and ugly and tasty, could Mui-mui pester. But Jeh-jeh was even better at snits. She nursed them well, letting them linger in the heart of her.

As she and her sister grew older, that didn't change. Jeh-jeh's snits were less tantrum in type, and more a cold silence, where she walked away from Mui-mui, heading into the cold waters of the asan mangroves to harvest the pods that grew from their roots. She could be

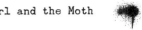

deaf, dumb, and blind if she wanted to when she was nursing a real snit, and she was all three when she heard her little sister calling out her name again and again one day, increasingly shrill in tone.

Jeh-jeh did not come. The cold of the water chilled her bones and her temper. Mui-mui stopped calling her, and she was finally left in peace. When she had had enough of the cold water and her basket was full of the asan pods, she headed back home.

She smelled it first—acrid smoke—before she turned the corner and saw that her house was ablaze and the door wide open. Jeh-jeh ran inside and was almost immediately overcome with black smoke and the roaring and popping of the fire.

Her father she found by stumbling over his legs. She felt her way to his ankles and dragged him out, her eyes as hot as cooked pennies, blinded and stinging with smoky tears.

She tried again for Mama and Mui-mui. But the air, by then, was as thick as black sand, scraping hot against her throat and squeezing breath from her lungs. It was all she could do to crawl back out, feeling her way to where her father lay on the dirt outside. She lay next to him, coughing, her eyes streaming with burning tears.

Her father was so still. She shook him, but he did not wake. Half-blind, she felt her way to his pulse. Her fingers encountered wet, torn flesh at his neck. And then higher, where his head should have been, nothing.

She scrambled back on her hands and knees and was sick. Her fingers found shards of wood, then the distinctive hard curve of jade, ridged over its body. The little jade charm. It was still cool to the touch.

The door. It had not been hanging open as she'd thought, but broken open—the wood hacked away. And all over the dark, splintered remains was a dusting of gold from the Emperor's moth.

If Mui-mui's cries had held a particular desperation that day which could have made her come back sooner, she had not heard it. Maybe her ears had been waterlogged. Maybe hers was a heart that was as shrivelled as a diseased asan pod that she could not recognise the sound of fear in her own sister's voice.

She thought of this over and over through the years, though she knew it was useless—turning the thought over in her mind so often it had become as smooth as polished jade, sliding effortlessly into her mind without warning and laying leaden upon her until her breath came short, and it was like she was in the burning house again.

It came again to her as she searched all through the cavern after making sure the moth was securely trapped beneath her basket. She ventured outside, squeezing through the narrow gap in the rock cautiously, but found nothing—no characters of death etched into the rock in gold, no sign of the Emperor's soldiers lying in wait.

Was it because she had no door? Mama had told her once that the moths were instructed by the mages to write the death orders on the doors of the condemned. But she had no door to speak of.

Back in her cavern, she lay down next to the upturned basket and studied the moth through the gaps in the weaving. The basket was so old the flaxen weaving was almost translucent in the dim light. The moth sat contentedly on the dirt floor under the basket, its antennae waving to make out its cage. When it shivered, the colour of its wings turned from silver to purple to green and back again, and a haze of gold dust rose, settling over the ground and the insides of its woven cage.

But it did not make the mark of death. It did not reveal her name.

She had run for all she was worth—run until her feet bled, and the tears and snot dragged down her face and dried into salty, sooty tracks that cracked when she moved her mouth to gulp in the cold night air.

Mama and Baba were gone. Mui-mui was gone. Her home was burned to ashes.

When she fled, she took virtually nothing with her—just the sopping, sooty clothes she had been wearing to dive amongst the mangrove roots, the basket of pods on her back, the sharp knife that she used to harvest them, and the little jade charm. She hid for a long time back in the marshes—watching for the Emperor's soldiers and chewing the

milky flesh of raw asan pods to quiet her rumbling stomach and keep herself awake.

They did not come.

She was too afraid of the soldiers to return to her home, even to bury her family. She moved further out into the swampy land, climbing through the dense tree branches to hide her tracks. Onwards she moved, farther and farther from home, until the asan mangroves thinned and new, unfamiliar trees surrounded her. The marshy waters congealed to thick mud, then solid earth.

She could not stay up in the trees forever, a stuck, singed, frightened bird. So she set her feet back on the ground and began to walk.

Four years was a long time to be alone, and an even longer time to be afraid. She had spent the first constantly on alert, taking in snatches of sleep during the day if she had a place to hide, and moving at night. She walked a long time in the dark. Maybe it was the black smoke of the fire, or maybe it was a consequence of crying so long. But it came that the greys and shadows of night were now stark outlines she could see clearly, like a line of the blackest of ink on aged paper. Daylight was now too bright for her and made her eyes water painfully, her tears still black with soot.

When she slept during the day, she dreamed of her father lying outside their house, abandoned, his headless body covered in flies and insects, then those eyeless, dancing maggots. There had been hardly anything of him when he was alive—he had been all lean, rangy muscle built from working the land, all of his padding from sitting at his desk studying magical texts worked off. In her dreams, his body would putrefy, flesh disappearing into the mouths of maggots, the liquid of him seeping into the land. After, his bones would scatter themselves as they saw fit—either through scavenging animals, or through the sheer force of gravity as they were released from the casing of cartilage and muscle to lie amongst the burned ruins of their old home.

And his head. By all that was sacred, his head.

She moved up the tall green hills, then down the other side and through the neighboring valley where the people looked like her but spoke another tongue she couldn't understand. She stayed away from them and ate what she could snatch and scrounge, stealing into empty houses that'd had their doors left unlocked.

Often, she thought of their old home's broken wooden door. She felt cheated by it. If her family were to be taken from her, at least leave their names for her to learn and remember them by. The part of her that was not utterly tired—a small, jade-cold part of herself that raged and raged, that was a storm in miniature that gathered slights and hoarded snits—hungered for her family's names and for the symbol of death, so that she could go through each of the Emperor's men, and carve out their names upon their flesh and take from them what had been taken from her.

She was afraid of that part of herself. And yet she could not wholly regret her anger. It had been what had saved her in the first place. She nursed it carefully. She was alive. Her parents and sister were not, but *she* was alive.

She came to the mountains. If she had not been left with her strange night sight after the fire, she would never have spotted the shadows and lines in its rock face and would have kept walking the nights over endlessly. But she saw the gap in the rocky cliff face, just wide enough to fit her body through. She had squeezed herself in, inching further and further into the heart of cold rock. The crack had opened into a hollow big enough for her to lie down in.

At last, she'd found a safe place to rest.

It had been five days since the moth arrived, and still the soldiers had not come. She was too tired to run, so she lay there beside the moth and waited. The moth rocked slowly in its cage, never making a single stroke of gold.

On the sixth day, she lifted the basket from the moth and set it aside. She gave it a little precious honey—stolen from the stinging wild bees—mixed with water, in the husk of an asan pod. Well, why not? She had begun to think of the moth fondly. She so rarely had guests—only the wind and black horned beetles paid visits, and one of those she ate if she was starving.

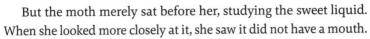

But the moth merely sat before her, studying the sweet liquid. When she looked more closely at it, she saw it did not have a mouth.

It was not expected to live so long, she realised. When the mages had shaped it from magic, they had not thought of it as a real, living creature in need of sustenance.

"Cruel," she told it. "Most cruel."

It stopped its rocking and peered at her face. She watched it back.

When she said nothing more, it resumed its rocking, antennae curling and uncurling as it tasted the air.

Sometimes she tested her memory.

She remembered the sign for *one*—a single horizontal stroke. Easy as breath. *Two* was a duo of strokes, one lying over the other, like the waterline above the marshy ground at low tide. *Three* was another horizontal line above that, the black of sky lined up to earth and water below.

Four was where her memory halted.

She had known it before. Her mother taught her before the purge. Mama taught her how to write her name, too. Not Jeh-jeh, but her *name*, and their name. Each stroke was herself. Each stroke was a line her ancestors had written before her—the old magic passed down along the generations, until the purge ended it.

She could not remember the sound of it, either. Mama told her once that she had been named after Porpor, whom they'd both missed so terribly. Mui-mui had still been just a baby then, and was curled asleep against her chest, a heavy, pleasant weight. She'd been on the edge of sleep herself when Mama came in to check on them. Her mother had kissed Mui-mui on her forehead first, then bent down to kiss her on the shell of her ear. By the time Mama stood, she'd been gifted with the whispering of Porpor's and her own name.

That was a long time ago now. Sometimes, she wondered if she dreamed it. She could not remember her mother's voice any longer. The marshy waters and black rasping smoke and long grinding time had conspired to wear it away from her memory. Only, sometimes, she thought she heard snatches of it in the wind that compelled her to turn without quite knowing what it was that called to her so.

"I knew it once," she told the moth. It lay on the ground next to her, listening patiently. It had been so long since she had someone to speak to that her throat hurt and her jaw ached from talking. The moth watched her, antennae twitching in sympathy.

"Sometimes, I hear fragments of it in my dreams." She yawned wide, her jaw cracking with the effort. She was so unutterably tired.

It was then that the moth launched itself at her. It covered almost all her face with its great fluttering wings, its antennae probing at her eyes and mouth. She could feel the stroke of them singeing her skin.

She batted it away, but it came at her again, flattening those fragrant, velvety wings against her cheeks and lips, those feathery fronds like hot sparks. Her left eye was filled with burning gold.

"Stop!" she cried, and the gold powder filled her mouth too—bitter and hot—the taste of death, she thought, if death could have a savour.

She ripped it from her face, all gentleness gone, and tore at its wings, tore it apart until there was nothing in her hands but gold dust and ripped velvet paper.

For the next few days, she burned with a fever that was like being in her burning home again. She dreamed terrible dreams, of giant moths cast out in flight, seeking their targets to bring them their deaths. Of headless soldiers, coming for her—the stumps of their necks crawling with dancing maggots. Her dreams were all in greys and golds—she saw the tops of trees, the forests in the dark night and early dawn, the moths moving so quickly and with such an air of magic to their being that even the hawks that watched with their sharp, predatory eyes were wary of snatching at them. The moths pulled at her from every direction—she went with each of them, all at once, her mind a confusion of images as the moths were sent north and west and east and south to seek their targets. And she saw the doors of their targets' homes, felt their bodies land upon them with such lightness, as if a mere breath upon a sleeping cheek, and, as they quivered, wings splayed to display their imperial colours, she shivered in heat and ice too. She learned to write the symbol for death, and each of the names of the condemned, every stroke careful and precise.

The thunder of soldiers' feet would come soon after, roaring like fire. And then their blades.

She woke sweated through and panting, choking on the taste of gold, her left eye weeping incessantly and sight blurred with gold. She swiped at her face, and her fingers came away shimmering with the colour. No matter how much she tried, gold clung to her skin. Her eyes stung with crying; her lips stung too.

She pulled the pieces of the moth together—poor paper wings, poor broken body—and when she unravelled the crumpled wings, she saw the strokes of magic hidden inside. She recognised the sign of death from her dreams. And she saw pieces of familiar strokes, half-forgotten from so long ago.

Her name. She had the start.

As she pieced the wings of the moth back together, she relearned it, each stroke a tone, each fold of paper the rustle of a syllable. She worked on, matching stroke to stroke to form her name, lining up the creases in the moth's tattered body and mending the torn paper with a little honey. She made the moth whole again, and gave it a mouth. When she was finished, it was a cool, weighty thing in her hands. She let her warmth seep into its wings and body and dripped morning dew and honey into its mouth slowly, until she had no more honey left. She fell asleep cradling the moth to her.

She woke to the scent of honey and wild sage, and the slow crawl of careful feet on her shoulder, up her neck. The moth. It reached her ear and stretched out its wings, and this time she heard the rustle of them, like soft, damp paper. Another testing stretch. Then, it fluttered its wings, shivering hard, and it seemed to her it was a kind of language, the vibrato of quivering speech echoing in the air. Again and again, the moth shook hard, and suddenly—like a puzzle unlocked—she understood its whispering wings.

Follow, it said. *Follow, Tailin.*

POC United

It was the first time in years she had heard her name spoken by anyone. The sound of it was a relief—a spell broken, a vital part of herself, missing so long, suddenly found and locked back into place, and the memory of her mother whispering to her came to her whole.

Of course. She was Tailin. That was what she was called.

And so, when the moth flitted into the air and out of her home cave, Tailin followed it.

The moth flew only at night, which suited Tailin well. Her eyes still burned, her left one in icy gold, her right weeping black tears in sympathy.

Sunlight was more blinding than ever, so she retreated into shade during the day. The moth lay on her face, shielding her eyes from the light, its feathery fronds stroking her forehead, like how Mama and Porpor used to gently thread their fingers through her hair when she was little, when they still called her by her true name.

When she cried, the moth flicked her tears from its wings gently, the tips of them patting her eyelids and cheeks. She cried harder at its motions. The moth's little feet skittered on its hold on her nose, and wrapped its wings entirely around her temples for purchase in a fragrant embrace. She felt the curled tip of its tongue lapping away the tears from her burning eyes.

She slept and dreamed of flight, of the moon pulling her on through the skies.

She woke when night came again, as it ever did, and the moth took flight. Tailin followed.

They came upon a pool of water in a forest clearing, so still the moon shone bright and round, as if it rested at the bottom of it. Beyond it, the forest floor bloomed with flowers of white and silver, so numerous they looked as if the clouds had descended, entangled with stars, and settled upon the earth.

In the water, Tailin saw her face—the strokes of the moth clinging to her in gold. One ran from the mop of her black hair, sweeping down from the amber skin of her temple, over her left eye. Another crossed her right cheekbone. And, below them, a slash of gold over her lips.

She had the mark of death on her face and the beginning strokes of her name.

The moth landed on her shoulder. *Look*, it said.

"I see. I see the mark you have left on me."

No. Look.

She lifted her gaze from her reflection to the field beyond. A breath of wind blew through, and masses of petals lifted into the air, whole blossoms tumbling through the wind, rustling like soft paper. She did not understand what she was seeing at first. But she caught the scent of something sweet and bitter, the fragrance so familiar now.

Moths. Not flowers at all. Thousands upon thousands littered the forest floor, discarded after completing their task. Even in death, they had not lost their iridescence or scent.

She caught one floating past, careful not to crush its wings. Without the life of magic, it was so light, nothing like the weight of the moth on her shoulder. Its antennae were tipped with gold. Its wings were tattered and translucent, like the lacy husks of leaves with just the veins remaining intact. But, within them, she could see the creases that had formed their wings and legs and antennae, each fold hiding the names of the dead, her people, written in the clasp of their bodies.

Tailin let her legs fold beneath her and sat down amongst the dead, her eyes wet with soot and gold.

"Yes, I see," she told the moth. "I see my people."

And Tailin set about remaking them.

Sarah LaBrie

ON WRITING

Wretched, wretched, and yet with good intentions.
—The Diaries of Franz Kafka, 1910–1913

Writing well is hard. All writers know this. So why don't we talk about it more? *But we do*, I hear you groan. *All writers do is complain*. Well, true. But it's also true that most of that complaining comes after said writer has achieved some modicum of success. The back pages of the *Best American Short Stories* anthologies, for example, are replete with different versions of one tale told over and over: facing constant rejection, a writer wrestles with the prospect of giving up, then a phone call comes at the last minute, telling her that everything she's ever dreamed of is suddenly about to take place.

When the prospect of failure lies just over the horizon, we don't like talking about our unfinished drafts, rejected submissions, or impossible-to-fix manuscripts quite as much. The well intentioned rejections from literary magazines and the "no" emails from agents—sure, they make great dinner party fodder after pub day, but not when we're still waiting for somebody, anybody, to recognize our hard work. Even in this, the era of "fail fast and fail often," for many writers, to admit to not having gotten there yet feels like acknowledging the very real possibility that we might not ever get there at all.

Which is, in some sense, ridiculous. No one expects a medical student to perform surgery correctly on his first try. And no corporate lawyer would be allowed to negotiate a merger without experience and years of law school behind her. Lawyers and doctors learn by doing. Writers feel we should already know. Proust never got an MFA. Mary Shelley wrote *Frankenstein* at twenty. Helen Oyeyemi wrote her first novel while she was still at Cambridge. And it's not as if we're the only people telling ourselves this. As the writer Tim Parks once put it in an essay for the *New York Review of Books*, "No one is treated with more patronizing condescension than the unpublished author or, in general, the would-be artist. At best he is commiserated. At worst mocked. He has presumed to rise above others and failed."[1]

Ambition is a delicate thing, and being mocked, condescended to, or, worse, pitied, feels bad. But I think we do ourselves a serious disservice by not talking more openly about what failing at writing feels like. By this, I mean the physical feeling of writing badly: the instinct that tells you when a prepositional phrase is wrenching your sentence in the wrong direction; the sense that comes upon a writer all at once that her entire career has beached itself upon a handful of paragraphs she just can't order correctly; the feeling that settles upon her, even as she hits "send" on a manuscript, that she just hasn't gotten it right, and that perhaps she never will.

That's why I was pleased, a few years ago, to hear the poet and academic Anne Carson, in conversation with *Bookworm* host Michael Silverblatt, speak honestly about her book, *Red Doc>*. The novel, the sequel to Carson's much loved *Autobiography of Red*, was highly anticipated and had already received heaps of critical praise and attention. Of it, Carson said the following:

> Yeah, I mean, I don't love it at all. I just...did it because I had determined to. And I don't think I even admire it—I shouldn't say that because of course it will cut down sales—but I can't think of a way I could have done this that would have seemed right at the end. It was just a matter of getting through it.

1. Tim Parks, "Writing to Win," *New York Review of Books* (January 2014).

Silverblatt expresses astonishment, saying to Carson, "I think it's not uncommon that a writer regards a particular work as an agony. Something to have been gotten through. But I have to tell you, this is the first time anyone has ever said so. I think that's amazingly honest."

"Oh darn," Carson responds. "I did it again."

On the one hand, this hesitance on the part of writers to speak about the difficulty of what we do makes sense. Writers aren't surgeons, and the hardships we face can, in the greater scheme of things, feel unimportant. Our friends and families are certainly tired of hearing about our issues, so why would we share them with strangers? If writing proves too difficult, we can always just give up and get real jobs, right? Too, this type of talk just adds more depressing substance to the conversation around an already depressing industry, one that's riddled with failure, rejection, budget cuts, underpaid adjuncting and publishing assistant jobs, and books ghostwritten for Internet celebrities getting all the attention while everyone else slowly starves.

For me, developing a regular writing practice in graduate school and after proved painful and elusive. I strained for months and years over pieces that would never see publication, while all my best stories tended to be completed in a matter of hours or in an afternoon. When writing those stories—the ones that eventually got published or caught the attention of editors and agents—I had a sense of having been carried by some type of wave that, once the work was finished, deposited me back on shore and disappeared without a trace. The stretches in between those waves were marked by terrible writing, weight gain, stress-related hair loss, and random crying. Never in any of my fiction workshops, in college, in graduate school, or beyond, was the cyclical and mercurial nature of this process, and the physical, mental, and social damage it could cause, ever mentioned. I wish it had been. It wouldn't have stopped me writing, but it would have made me feel less alone, less certain that at some point down the line it would simply not be worth it anymore, and that I would have to give up.

Now, when I teach, I assign my students the *Paris Review* interviews—that magazine's series of lengthy in-person discussions with famous writers—for every author we read. I have my students read

POC United

James Baldwin's famous essay "Stranger in the Village," in all its abundant lyricism, alongside the conversation in which he calls writing "a terrible way to make a living," adding, "I find writing gets harder as time goes on. I'm speaking of the working process, which demands a certain amount of energy and courage…and a certain amount of recklessness. I don't know, I doubt whether anyone—myself at least—knows how to talk about writing. Perhaps I'm afraid to."[2]

Rather than finding these words depressing, my students tend to find some measure of relief in an understanding that everyone, even Baldwin, struggled. I also have them read relevant entries from Susan Sontag's journals (*"My will is more flabby than it's ever been before. Let this be the dip before the upswing."*[3]) or Franz Kafka's (*"That I have put aside and crossed out so much, indeed almost everything I wrote this year, that hinders me a great deal in writing."*[4]). My personal favorite is a June 1910 diary entry of Kafka's, which begins, in his characteristically upbeat tone, *"slept, awoke, slept, awoke, miserable life."*[5] All of these lines appear in pages composed before these authors became household names or had any concept that they would be, when they were simply struggling towards the creation of work that was meaningful to them.

What I want to do with my students is to demystify the process. To show them, as I wish someone had shown me when I was very young, that writers aren't gods alone in a room, pumping out perfectly metered prose from the time they sit down at their desks until it's time to go down to the bar. Writing is a lot of frustrating, hard work completed over time. Whether you're good at it or talented winds up mattering less, in the end, than the ability to keep doing it, even in the face of your own pain and the world's potential apathy.

We're embarrassed to talk about the difficulty of writing, but we shouldn't be. Writing is supposed to be hard. It's good that it's difficult.

2. "James Baldwin, The Art of Fiction No. 78," *The Paris Review Interviews Book II* (New York: Picador, 2007), 251–252.

3. Susan Sontag, *Reborn: Journals and Notebooks,* 1947–1963 (New York: Farrar, Straus and Giroux, 2009), 103.

4. Franz Kafka, *Diaries:* 1910–1923 (New York: Schocken Books Inc, 1948, 1949), 30.

5. Ibid, 14.

Sarah LaBrie

Eating. Sleeping. Being on the Internet. Watching television. These gestures of passive consumption come easily to most of us for a reason. The difficulty of writing well is a key element of its importance. If it isn't difficult, at least at first, there's a genuine possibility that it's not being done very well.

A more pertinent question might be: why do writers continue to write at all? A professor of mine once said that it's because we don't want to die. I used to think there was something to that, but now I think it has more to do with what happens on the flip side of writing badly, by which I mean the series of clicks that happen when the words fall onto the page exactly the way they're supposed to, the pleasant, low-level madness that starts to take hold when the work is going well, when coincidences abound and everything anyone says takes on a greater significance, the whole world bathed in light.

At the same time, it's possible that the answer is something simpler, and that Kafka landed on it in his journals many years before I did: *"The burning electric light, the silent house, the darkness outside, the last waking moments, they give me right to write even if it be only the most miserable stuff. And this right I use hurriedly. That's the person I am."*[6]

6. Ibid, 39.

Cynthia Alessandra Briano

TO MARIA, MI FEA, LOVE, JESSE

Instead of the salmon, we'll serve little tacos,
just like you like, and we'll make
our day
your day.

Norman and Bertha will observe at a cool,
feline distance, so as to not make

your eyes tear, and I'll think on how
it was sheer love all those nights
that made you sleep by my side
with an itchy throat

and an ice pack
over your face.
Together, we'll
overcome anything, you'll see, even allergies—

our love is stronger
than cat hair,

and, thanks to Benadryl, even far
ahead into my life, when loving you
has made me more than a niño,

Graffiti

you'll still let me curl
up in your

lap bed arms calves toes neck...

I've decided
that on our day, instead of having you
walk up to me
as is tradition, I'll come up

behind you,
and we can reenact

the tap on the shoulder with which this all began:
Hi, I'm Jesse.
Hi, I'm Maria.

I don't remember the subject—history, I think—
but I remember the seat
in front of me with you

in it, and I think on
what it is to begin

a pivotal thing in my life
with such simplicity.

Cynthia Alessandra Briano

TO JESSE, LOVE, MARIA GUADALUPE A.

The answer is that we won't translate
our terms of endearment
into English, that's all. You can call me
Ugly
if you want—Fea, or
Mi Fea or Lupita La Fea.

My cousin, Fatso,
can vouch for our love despite
the name calling.

I reckon the slight is permissible,
if even the cats
perk and arch
when you greet them before anything else,
even if it's late, your made-up
dance and song

in that high-pitched girly
falsetto and you

prancing prettily around the room:
"Hey little Norman, stupid little cat..."

The answer is that we'll speak in tongues
and parables, the way you did that day

on my porch, "Close your eyes,"
you said, "I'm gonna tell you a story..."

You went on, something happened,
  "and then it started to rain..."

there were jasmine petals in your pocket,
and over me your fist opened like a cloud.

You had pulled them from that bush that always smelled nice
when we walked from your house to mine.

We can map out my girlhood on the streets
of Huntington Park, so much

of my girlhood is with you. That day
on the other side of the train tracks,
behind the entrance of that office building
on Randolph Street, nowhere

in particular, just some grass and a tree,
you took pictures of me. I remember

your eyes on me and how private
your camera.

A few blocks down, there is the site
of our first date: that old unyellow doughnut shop

on State Street. Were we fifteen?
I hadn't seen you in a long time, I didn't really

recognize you, you had had a growth spurt,
and you'd cut your red hair, and you were skinny,
and you had glasses now, and you weren't

Little Jesse anymore, but you still ate sorbet and
were sheepish when they played *Chapel of Love.*
Were we fifteen? Years later,

in Puerto Vallarta, at La Chata Bar, with the trio playing,
you asked the waiter to move the tables so we could
dance. I don't remember the song you requested,

but I remember being embarrassed
in the same way you blushed at the doughnut shop, in the
    same way

my stomach still leaps the way your fat cats never do
when you pick me up for a date,

I imagine you coming to me, tall and timely
even though you don't start
to get ready until there's twenty
minutes left before you have to leave,

I imagine you reaching into your pocket

fisting your hand into a cloud.

Tamika Thompson

IN A HARD MAN'S TOWN

Malaika hopped down from Daddy's truck, refusing his attempt at a goodbye kiss on her cheek. She'd been looking forward to a weekend of hot chocolate at Sweet Steel Soda Shop and dominoes near the crackle of the fireplace, but Daddy had picked up an extra shift at work. He was bailing again.

"No sugar for me, no sugar for you." She poked out her bottom lip, turned to make sure he saw it, and then pressed against her big brother and his oversized backpack on the sidewalk. Her tongue found the gap between her bottom teeth where, the previous day, a baby tooth had fallen out. The firm flesh with the missing root was sore still and tasted of salty blood.

"Y'all know them scounds out at the plant like to call in sick on Fridays." Daddy always had an excuse. "Bazooka Joe for both of you when I'm done." Promising Malaika and Malcolm pieces of bubblegum did little for her disappointment when that gum was all she had to look forward to now.

She stepped forward and slammed the door hard enough to make the glass rattle in the frame.

"Keep those butts on the rug until bedtime, M and M. You hear me?" That was Daddy's parting warning as he sped off looking hurt and frustrated.

"Whatever." Malcolm climbed the front steps and only spoke when Daddy was out of earshot. "Let's go out back and play fetch with Knight."

Malaika's walk became a skip, because she thought that was the best idea ever.

Still in their school uniforms, she and Malcolm stood on their back porch, a deck that Daddy built using wood he'd chopped himself. Thick clouds blocked the afternoon sun and made the day breezy. Mango-colored leaves were scattered across the grass and the garden of cucumbers and collards. The narrow, red peppers nearby—which Malaika figured were probably super-spicy—resembled the ones Daddy had cooked into the pot of chili waiting on the stove. Even though "M and M" were breaking a rule, which could mean being grounded or worse, it felt good to be outside with an entire weekend ahead of them.

She expected for Knight to jump up on the chain-link fence of his pen, with his claws jutting out of the gate's diamonds, whining, sticking out his sandpaper tongue, and dog-laughing because he was so happy to see them. But, as they passed the twelve-foot elm tree and snapped off three low branches for their game of fetch, the yard was silent.

"Knight?" Her breath floated before her face. A bitter October wind burned her cheeks. Something felt off, but she didn't know what. Maybe they should have listened to Daddy and stayed inside.

When Knight's furry face didn't appear at the gate, Malcolm looked the same way he did when Malaika had choked on a wad of gum and needed his hard rib-hug to cough it back out.

They arrived at Knight's pen, a four-by-four square enclosure with hay on the floor and a straw bed, but Knight wasn't lapping up water or nibbling on leftover ribs smothered in Daddy's homemade barbecue sauce.

Malcolm shook and rattled the gate. No answer. The pen smelled like Knight's poop, but he was nowhere. Not near Daddy's red Monte Carlo, sitting on four concrete bricks in their garage, either.

"Where'd he go?"

Malcolm didn't answer, she was sure, because he thought she asked "too many danged questions all the time."

Malcolm scurried in and came out of the garage with his ten-speed and her Minnie Mouse cruiser, his bike ticking as he walked it to the gate at the head of their driveway.

"Malcolm! We can't ride when Daddy ain't home." Daddy wasn't so much worried about the gangs in their neighborhood. He had already threatened the Mackenzie Boys by showing up to their spot at the park with his hunting rifle and asking them whether they had ever heard what happened to their missing member. He didn't want Malcolm and Malaika prancing up and down the streets because then they'd be mannish like the "ruffians" on the block, who cussed, smoked, and drank, when they needed to be in the house with their "noses in them books."

"Yeah. But when Daddy ain't at home, who's in charge?"

Malaika was seven. Malcolm was twelve, but he acted as if he were twenty. She put her tongue against that spot in her mouth again where the tooth had become lodged in a slice of apple and snapped out. She remembered the pain and shock of it. But each time her tongue found the opening, it was a little less sore. She folded her arms across her chest, and stamped her right foot to let him know she was staying put. Though she was mad at Daddy for ditching, she wasn't breaking a second rule because Malcolm said so. Especially when Daddy had promised gum.

"Look, Malaika. It'll just be for ten minutes and it's only because we need to find Knight before the sun goes down."

In the decade Knight had been in their family, he'd never left home.

"Think maybe somebody kidnapped him?"

Malcolm squinted at her question but didn't answer.

"But, why would they, Malcolm? Knight is old as Methuselah. Who else would want him?"

She stared at the empty bits of hay in Knight's pen. Whether somebody wanted Knight or he'd wandered off, the dog was sure enough gone. Malcolm was right, and she hated that. They climbed on their bikes' cold seats. Gooseflesh sprouted on her neck and arms as she trailed behind Malcolm out of the gates, down the driveway, and onto the forbidden street.

The way Malcolm told it, when he was two, Mother went to the pound and came out with Knight, a strange-looking, black-and-white mix of German spitz, poodle, and cocker spaniel, with hair for days and a tail the mutt liked to beat on their wooden floor like a drum. He often rolled on his back beneath the coffee table, making it impossible for them to rub his belly. He'd snort and dog-laugh when they'd tap on the glass above him.

Malcolm told Malaika that he was nine when Mother returned to her family in Honduras. After Mother left, Knight had crouched at the foot of Mother and Daddy's bed licking Mother's pink house slippers. Malcolm started talking about Mother all the time—how she used to take him downtown to train with professional baseball players, how she would cart him to Eastern Market to pick out a live chicken. That story always made Malaika's flesh crawl, but Malcolm said he thought it was cool that Mother would kill, clean, and cook the meat herself before serving and eating it.

Malaika could barely conjure up an image of Mother. She remembered Mother's lollipop-colored dress that flowed to her ankles and the way that Mother zipped about life like a wind-up toy, but if it weren't for the snapshot of Mother smiling and leaning against Daddy at the drive-ins, Malaika wouldn't know what her mother's face looked like. Malaika often caught Daddy standing in front of the framed photo that still hung on their dining room wall, just staring at the two of them sitting on the hood of his car. One time she even saw him caress the image right where Mother's hair fell to her shoulders, but Malcolm told her that Daddy was probably just wiping away a smudge.

A week after Mother had split, Malcolm said he took Knight as his own, hanging out in the bedroom with the dog during the day and returning him to the hay-lined pen near the garage at night, so Daddy wouldn't "pitch a fit" when he got home. Daddy didn't allow animals "with they damn fleas" to live in the house with his kids and the food that he worked hard to put on the table. Daddy had grown up on a Georgia farm and told them that pets were supposed to earn their keep—"hunt, fetch, guard, something!" According to Daddy, Knight was like a black hole that sucked up his extra dough.

"We black," Daddy would say. "Our dogs ain't family members." Malcolm would chime in, "Half-black," and Daddy would give him a half-grin and smack him on the back of the head. Malcolm's head was red all the time from Daddy swatting him there, but Malcolm never seemed hurt by it. Malaika could feel it though and would touch the back of her head as if Daddy had swatted her instead.

The first stop was Mr. Conrad's house, made of green-and-white-striped aluminum siding that looked like a big ol' crooked lawn chair. The homes on Mackenzie Street mostly belonged to Detroit's auto-plant workers, tire-shop workers, body-shop workers, engine-part workers, and their secretary wives. It was just after three. Most of the grown-ups were still at work, but the kids rode bikes and played basketball in the middle of the street with a bottomed-out bucket for a hoop.

And then there were the folks that Daddy called "no-good scounds," who broke into homes, stole rides, jacked cars, and lifted license-plate tags and hubcaps. Daddy told Malcolm and Malaika that they were easy to identify because "scounds" often sat on their front porches "talking too loud and smoking reefa."

Because of those folks, Malcolm and Malaika slept with a baseball bat and screwdriver near their beds when Daddy wasn't home. Luckily, Knight was like an alarm. Anybody came near the house while Daddy worked evenings, Knight would bark for a full hour, gnaw off the pen's latch, and tear into the person's ankles if he had to.

"Excuse us, Mr. Conrad, you seen Knight?" Boys on the block usually made fun of Malcolm because he and Malaika went to "white folks' school," and they said Malcolm talked like he had a "stick up his butt." Malaika thought they also made fun of him because, with light brown skin, dusty blonde hair, and prominent cheekbones, he looked more like a girl than a boy and was the only black person around with freckles. Truth be told, he looked just like Mother in that photo on the dining-room wall.

"Can't say that I has." Mr. Conrad never rose from the Mustang hood his head was buried under. A mechanic on disability from a Ford dealership, Mr. Conrad tinkered with an army of hooapties parked in his backyard, driveway, and across his uneven front lawn. The whole place smelled like a gas station. And, since Mr. Conrad was always outside, he knew everything that happened on the street. He kept a radio on his front porch tuned to 1960s Motown hits even though everyone else listened to WJLB, which had moved on to 1990s R&B like Bell Biv DeVoe. One night, some of the Mackenzie Boys had spray-painted Mr. Conrad's garage with gang tags while he was sleeping. Mr. Conrad had tracked them all down, dragged them kicking and screaming to his garage, belted their behinds with cowhide fresh from his waist, and, instead of making them paint over the writing like the other neighbors had, he told them to put some "real art up on them walls. Something that was worth looking at." People from the neighboring streets often walked over just to see the spray-painted images of Dr. Martin Luther King, Jr., Angela Davis, Malcolm X, and Assata Shakur. After that, Daddy, who was suspicious of everyone all the time, softened to Mr. Conrad and told Malaika and Malcolm that they could trust Mr. Conrad to help out if there was an emergency, but they were still not allowed to go inside Mr. Conrad's house or accept anything from him. Especially anything that needed digesting.

"Knight's missing, sir." Malcolm sounded as if he wanted to cry. She wanted to remind him not to act like a "sissy" outside, where he could get jumped. "If you see or hear him, can you give us a holler?"

"Shole will." Mr. Conrad raised his head, blew a small bubble of gum, and stared at them. He was Santa in blue overalls, with a stomach like a bowling ball and a scar that cut across the bridge of his nose. Malaika liked Mr. Conrad. She liked anyone who chewed gum all of the time.

Remembering Daddy's promise, she followed Malcolm back to their bike seats. She couldn't wait 'til Daddy got home with that gum, even though she would pretend to still be mad.

Just before they pushed off, Mr. Conrad spoke softly. "Ya Daddy know y'all out here riding around?"

A gold Impala turned onto the head of the block and zoomed down the street at about thirty miles per hour, a sure sign that the car did not belong in the neighborhood. Kids scattered. One threw a dirty Nerf ball, and the foam torpedo struck the car's back window and bounced off.

Drivers who knew better went about five miles an hour. First-timers floored it like this fool, bottoming out their cars as they banged the asphalt and flew over soccer-ball-sized potholes.

"He wouldn't mind, sir." Malaika ignored the Fool Impala as it clunked up and down in front of them then screeched around the corner. "We're not being mannish or nothing. We just looking for Knight."

Mr. Conrad reached in the greasy pocket of his overalls and pulled out four pieces of Bazooka Joe. Her mouth watered as she stared at the gum in his hand. She always saved her comic-strip wrappers, lining them up on her dresser between her hair bows and animal-shaped earrings. She'd have to hide these wrappers. Malcolm thought the comics were childish and discarded them as soon as he popped those red squares in his mouth.

"Girl, you look more and more like your Daddy every day." Mr. Conrad smiled. "Got his tight eyes and high cheekbones. Must be the Indian in your family."

"Yes. Creek Indian." Malaika eyed that gum, her mouth watering. "And, guess what. I lost a tooth yesterday." She opened her mouth and pointed to the gap on the bottom.

"You don't say?" Mr. Conrad smiled and seemed genuinely impressed.

She reached for the treats, but Malcolm snatched all four pieces and tucked them in his pants pocket.

Mr. Conrad nodded, his face growing serious, as if he'd crossed a line and Malcolm had just pushed him back behind it. "Lemme ask you a question, son. How old's your dog?"

"Twelve, like Malcolm."

Malcolm cut his eyes at her and clenched his jaw, letting her know she'd spoken three too many times already.

"And when you saw that your dog was missing, was his bowls still where you thought they'd be?"

"No, sir." Malcolm seemed hopeful when he answered, but two seconds rolled by, and then Malcolm lowered his head as if something had passed between him and Mr. Conrad, though whatever the something was, it had passed right on over Malaika's head. Mr. Conrad put his thick, white work gloves on and patted Malcolm on the shoulder.

"Right, son. Exactly as I thought. Y'all two go on home now. Talk it out with your Daddy when he gets back. But ain't no way I'm gone let y'all ride up and down these streets when your Daddy ain't home. Especially with these fools speeding 'round here. Go on. Don't need to look all pitiful neither."

Mr. Conrad ducked his head back under the hood, letting them know that the conversation was over and that they'd better return their bikes to the garage, take their mannish butts to the living room rug, and wait for Daddy.

"What's the big deal about the bowls being gone?" Malaika's bike didn't tick like Malcolm's ten-speed, but the chain creaked as she moved it into the garage and leaned it against the wall, careful not to disturb the bucket of dirt and worms sitting atop Daddy's tackle box. "Maybe Knight chased off a crackhead again and got lost. Somebody'll bring him back."

"Let's just go eat." Malcolm's voice was still low and sad.

"Okay. But, first, I want my gum. You broke two rules. Now it's my turn."

Malcolm cocked his head to the side as if he'd forgotten about the treat until she mentioned it. "No gum from Mr. Conrad."

"I want my gum. You chew yours too. Ain't nothing wrong with Mr. Conrad and his gum and Daddy knows it. Daddy's just being scaranoid."

"Stop trying to use big words you don't understand."

"What big words?"

"Scaranoid?"

"That's not a big word."

"I know. Because scaranoid is not a word. And you're not getting the stupid gum."

She felt a cry coming on, but she fought it. Malcolm never talked harsh to her. If the gum was making him hate her, then she didn't want it none. "Why you mad at me?"

Malcolm removed the gum from his pocket, walked over to the garbage can, and lifted the lid.

He froze in front of the open trash. Staring into that bin, his fist tight around those four pieces of gum, he dropped the top on the ground. The tin cover crashed to the concrete, banging loud enough to echo on the blocks around them. A bird shrieked in the tree and flapped away. Even though the trash lid had come to rest, Malaika could still hear the tinny noise, as if a ghost were carrying on the clanging. She'd never heard Malcolm scream or raise his voice before. She didn't even know that his voice could go so high. He covered his mouth with his gum-filled fist, but his screaming continued.

"Malcolm?" She crept closer to the can, wanting to know what his screams were about, but not sure that she wanted to look.

"Get back, Malaika!" His nose and cheeks were red. He pushed against her stomach, backing her up until her shoulders pressed against the pen where Knight should have been.

Mr. Conrad came crashing through their gate like a linebacker, closing the distance between him and Malcolm faster than she thought Mr. Conrad had been able to run. "Boy? What's wrong?"

Malcolm was still paralyzed at the trash can. Mr. Conrad peered inside slowly, then he picked the lid off of the ground and slammed it back onto the can. Malcolm's wails stopped.

Mr. Conrad put his hands on his hips, and he and Malcolm stared down at the can. She wished that she and Malcolm had've just sat on that rug and watched *Diff'rent Strokes* or *Good Times* re-runs. She wished they had've just minded Daddy. Whatever was in that trash can had made the air stink like fertilizer and cow manure. The trash man had already come the day before, so it would be smelly like that for a whole week.

"Did he—" Malcolm was hysterical. "Did he?"

"I told y'all to go in the house. See? This wouldn't have happened if you had've just listened to me when I told you."

Mr. Conrad opened the back door and shooed them inside. The gum fell out of Malcolm's hand and landed on the ground. Mr. Conrad picked up the wrapped gum pieces and reluctantly put them back in his pocket. When Malaika and Malcolm were inside, he slammed the door behind them.

"And don't come back out!"

The black television screen seemed to be watching them as if she and Malcolm were the show. Malcolm sat on the rug with his chin on his knees, staring into the powered-off television. He wouldn't let her ask him "not one question" nor pat his hand to console him. Even though their living room looked warm, with its thick brown curtains and couch cushions, chunky like marshmallows, the entire main floor of their two-story house was frosty. She dozed off on the rug next to him, the blast of heat from the vent as her blanket.

In the middle of the night, Malcolm tapped her shoulder. She woke and sat, stiff and straight, staring at the clock on the mantle that said 12:30 AM. Daddy was turning his key in the front door.

Daddy's hip must have been hurting him again, because he limped as he entered, a gust of cold air trailing him until he closed the door. He usually had posture like a soldier, but his broad shoulders sloped forward. His head didn't reach to the top of the door this time. He seemed to be carrying the extra shift on his back as he slowly removed his coat.

Stepping into the living room and dropping his cooler near the tree-shaped floor lamp, Daddy snapped, "What y'all still doing up?" His nose was red and his steel-toed boots were wet with drizzle.

"Did you bring the gum?" Malaika asked, so happy to see him that she'd forgotten to be mad.

Malcolm gave her that shut-up look.

"I said, 'what y'all doing up?'" Daddy's voice was harsh that time, as his eyes fell squarely on Malcolm.

Tamika Thompson

"Knight." His chin resting on his chest, Malcolm looked deranged.

"What about him?" Daddy's voice didn't have an edge that time. He stroked his beard twice, thinking, softening.

"Why didn't you tell us?"

Daddy looked away and removed his sweater. His expression was embarrassed-looking, the way he'd appeared when Malaika had asked him where babies come from.

"I'm the adult. You're the child." Daddy's tone was lighter, but he stared into the dining room, beyond the oak table, and to the kitchen.

She took Malcolm's hand, twice the size of hers and calloused, hoping that whatever had him going would end. She didn't want him arguing with Daddy and messing up her piece of Bazooka Joe. She didn't want him arguing with Daddy, period.

Malcolm removed his glasses. He wiped at his eyes. Did he have eye boogers, or was he crying again?

"You thought we wouldn't notice?"

"I ask you questions, boy. You don't ask me questions. Go to bed."

Daddy headed for the kitchen, where he always ate dinner and drank freshly squeezed lemonade before sprawling out fully-dressed on the couch until it was time to either take them to school or go to another of his jobs.

"I see why she left." Malcolm's voice was flat and low like a grown-up's, and, when he stood and held his arms tight against his sides, he looked like the twenty-year-old he always pretended to be.

Daddy whipped around so fast she thought that he was going to knock Malcolm's "hard-headed self" onto his "soft ass" like Daddy always threatened but had never done.

"You are mean and cruel." Large balls of tears ran down Malcolm's cheeks and clung to his chin, coming together as one fat droplet.

"You are toeing an ass-whooping, boy, disrespecting me in a house I pay for."

"Mean and cruel. Ignored her all the time. Never had a nice thing to say to her. And now Knight?"

Malaika needed Malcolm to stop crying. Malcolm's crying would make her cry. What had Daddy done? Given Knight away? Maybe

Daddy had sold their dog. Whatever Daddy had done, Malcolm needed to cut it out. Daddy and Malcolm couldn't be fighting each other. They just couldn't.

"Your mama was in the streets and carrying on."

"That's a lie!" Malcolm's voice cracked.

Malaika tugged on her ponytails, praying that the two people she loved more than the gum would stop fighting. Her chest tightened. Her palms were clammy. She just wanted to go to bed.

"Is it? You think professional baseball players train bow-legged kids for free? Down south, she would have been popped in the mouth for all of that ho-hopping. She should have been grateful that all I did was ignore her."

"You won't lie about Mother!" Malcolm walked up on Daddy.

Malaika grabbed Malcolm's arm, because the last time she'd seen him like this, he'd knocked a fifth-grader in the nose and sent the kid to the hospital for calling Malaika a "no-Mama-havin' mongrel."

Daddy placed his hand on Malcolm's head and palmed it like a basketball. Malcolm slapped at Daddy's massive arm, but the grip was unbreakable. Daddy always said he hated spanking them. He usually swatted them once on their tushies and that was it. It had been two years since he'd spanked Malcolm, but now spanking would have been the better option.

"I'm so mean and cruel? Then take your broke ass out there on the streets and feed yourself. Put clothes on your own back. Find a thousand dollars to send yourself to that sadiddy Catholic school. Then tell me how mean I am. Wanna throw your mother in my face? Tell me this. Did she buy one bag of dog food, one vet appointment, one worm treatment?"

Malcolm came to Daddy's chin, but they were so close that if he were taller, they'd be nose-to-nose now.

"So you threw Knight in the trash?" Malcolm shouted.

Malaika let go of Malcolm's arm and touched the back of her head because that's where she felt the sting. As if he or Daddy had slapped her there. She crumpled to the floor, her legs folded under her bottom. Her tongue found the gap in her gums. The area was no longer sore.

The salty blood taste was gone. She pressed her tongue into the opening, trying to get the pain to arrive, but it wouldn't. She wished the baby tooth were still in her mouth so that she could use this moment to rip it out. The walls and ceiling seemed to tip sideways and then righted. She was certain she was going to throw up.

"Don't say that, Malcolm! Don't say—" She covered her ears with her hands. She didn't notice the heat of her tears until they'd landed on the bertha collar of her uniform top and soaked through to her neck. "Don't. Don't. Don't!" She wanted to shout loud enough for the whole neighborhood to hear, though with her ears covered she could only hear her scream inside her head. She covered her eyes. Continued to scream the way that Malcolm had in front of that trash can. "Don't! Don't!"

She repeated "don't" what seemed like a hundred times and didn't stop until she felt Malcolm's hand on her arm. He pulled her to him, hugged her, but never took his eyes off of Daddy.

She buried her face in Malcolm's stomach, her forehead on his bony chest, and she held him around his back, wishing that she could be Velcroed to his side like this so that he could never let her go. Her head rose and fell against his belly as the air burst in and out of his lungs. He talked through a cry.

"Mean."

"You done with this charade?" Daddy asked.

She lifted her head. Daddy tried to sound annoyed, but his cheeks and nose were crimson, and tears like tiny diamonds sat in the corners of his eyes. Maybe he was as hurt by Malcolm's anger as she was.

"I ain't gonna talk about this no more, Malcolm. Ya hear me? You getting all emotional over a dog!"

She looked at Malcolm. He glared at Daddy still, but he held her tight.

"Cruel." Malcolm poked out his chest trying to seem older and larger than he was. And that one gesture made Malaika feel that he was his real age again.

"What you want me to do, Malcolm?" One of those diamonds got bigger in the corner of Daddy's eye, but it didn't fall. "He was old. He died. I had to pick y'all up from school. I had to go to work. I told y'all before about keeping animals as pets and giving 'em names and whatnot. Soft. That's what you are. Y'all are soft in a hard man's town."

"Loving ain't soft." Malcolm whispered through huffs.

"Say what you want. You'll learn. Just like I learned. But that's the last time you gon' talk back to me, boy. The last time. Now I ain't gon' tell y'all again. Go. To. Bed!"

And with that, Daddy was in the kitchen, snatching open the refrigerator and pounding it closed. Banging open the drawers. Clinking a utensil around the insides of a glass jar. Slamming the cabinets open and closed. Even the faucet he thumped on and off, the water sounding like a high-pitched chant as it filled a pot.

As she and Malcolm climbed the stairs, she wanted to forget their trashcan. She didn't want to think of Knight's body twisted up with their rotten food and crusted over nose tissues that would get tossed in the back of the garbage truck.

She imagined Daddy finding Knight dead, picking him up, and carrying him across their yard. She imagined him opening the can, but she couldn't picture him dumping Knight in there. Daddy must have been so sad to do it. He must have felt awful driving to school to pick them up. That's why Daddy never said nothing to them about it. Daddy hadn't had the heart to tell them that Mother had left either. They had heard about it from Mr. Conrad, who had seen Mother loading her suitcases into the trunk of a car that had come down the street driving a little too fast.

"Malcolm, where do the garbage men take the trash?"

Daddy must have heard her, because, after she spoke, he stopped knocking stuff around in the kitchen. She imagined those diamond tears falling from his eyes now that no one could see him.

"You ask too many questions." Malcolm's voice was soft, as if whatever fire had been in him moments ago had been put out.

When they woke in the morning, at the foot of Daddy and Mother's bed, having been too tired to continue the walk down the hall to their room, Daddy was already off to his second job at the body shop. He'd draped Big Mama's quilt over Malcolm and Malaika, and, on top of that toasty blanket, he'd placed two pieces of Bazooka Joe gum.

Malaika woke Malcolm, handed him a piece, and ripped hers open. The sugar burst on her tongue so quickly that the watering of her mouth ached, but she chomped away until the wad was no longer sweet. She could have taken both pieces, but that wouldn't have been right.

Malcolm had crust in his eyes. He gave her a half-grin when he opened his gum, examined it like his difficult trigonometry problems, and popped it in his mouth. She blew a bubble with hers and elbowed him, telling him to blow one as well. He wouldn't. He chewed it just long enough to get all of the sugar out, and then he spit it back in the wrapper without reading the comic strip, turned on his side, and went back to sleep.

She stared at his back, listening to him snore. She wished she could hear Knight howling in the yard. But the only sounds outside were bird chirps and Mr. Conrad's radio, tuned to the Four Tops's "Standing in the Shadows of Love." When there was no more sugar, she spit out her gum and placed the wet blob in the wrapper. She'd throw these comics away. Malcolm was right—lining up the colored paper on her dresser was childish.

"See that? Daddy bought us the gum, Malcolm." She closed her eyes. She loved being able to sleep as long as she wanted on Saturday mornings. She wished Daddy could sleep in some mornings too. "Not Mother, but Daddy. Daddy bought us the gum. Even Mr. Conrad gave us some gum. But not Mother. Okay?"

Malcolm was silent, but his snoring didn't start up again. He'd heard her. She imagined him apologizing to Daddy for all the mean things he'd said and Daddy saying sorry too. Or maybe they'd be nice, but say nothing about the argument. Malcolm had better do something to let Daddy know they were all right. Or she might not never share gum with Malcolm again.

Kay Ulanday Barrett

WHILE LOOKING AT PHOTO ALBUMS

Christmas Eve, 2016

Before everyone died – in my family – first definition I learned
was – my mother's maiden name, ULANDAY – which literally
means – of the rain – and biology books remind us – the pouring
has a pattern – has purpose – namesake means release – for my
mother, meant flee – meant leave – know exactly what parts of
you – slip away – drained sediment of a body – is how a single
mama feels – on the graveyard shift – only god is awake – is where
my – family banked itself – a life rooted in rosaries – like nuns in
barricade – scream – People Power – one out of five – leave to a
new country – the women in my family hone – in my heart – like
checkpoints – which is what they know – which is like a halt – not to
be confused for – stop – which is what happened to my ma's breath –
when she went home – for the last time – I didn't get to – hold her
hand as she died – I said I tried – just translates to – I couldn't make
it – in time – I tell myself – ocean salt and tear salt – are one and
the same – I press my eyes shut – cup ghost howl – cheeks splint
wood worn – which is to say – learn to make myself a harbor –
anyway – once I saw a pamphlet that said – what to do when your
parent is dead – I couldn't finish reading – but I doubt it informs the
audience – what will happen – which is to say – you will pour your
face & hands – & smother your mother's scream on everything – you
touch – turn eyelids into oars – go, paddle to find her.

Kay Ulanday Barrett

RHYTHM iS A DANCER, AGAIN.

#ForOrlando

When the responders came to a nightclub in Orlando,
they announced   *If you are still alive, raise your hand.*

Meanwhile,   I was asleep in a bed I never thought I would have.
People like us are used to lonely, are used to sobbing   so hard

that homes are like unfathomable dreams,   we search for
the rescue of safety in our own skin and reasons to just hold

someone's hand,   to just find a job that doesn't
call us by the wrong name, to just find ourselves lost in music.

Earlier that night, people didn't get to leave the dance floor.
What is the beat of bullets,   when we are too used to percussion
      already?

Cusses & threats beat at the seams of our skin, of course
salvation is to tut & tick   on our own terms and tears are but

dance sweat so as the gunshots from the balcony seared the air,
there were boys holding hands   with other boys   for the
      first time

which then became their last time,   and there were others trying
to forget a hard day to the lilt of limbs, at the lip of a bottle,

there were strobe lights that could've been falling stars   but
instead   they were bodies.

Before we die,   some of us are already dead to family photos,
our own blood kin close their eyes to us like caskets.

In a club, there was a young person or three, singing aloud,
who thought   *This my favorite song,*   a palm up to the air
        and the only

place that was safe became barrage, glass shards, their
friend's blood turned blanket.   The next morning, I couldn't stop

crying and I will tell you,   we've been crying a long time.
We've lit candles at vigils like it's as everyday as breathing.

We know the choreography of loss.   If there are no prayers
        possible, understand
moments before there were claps praising the dip of a
        harmony,   then nothing.

This isn't a shining beacon of a new reality. There is no epiphany.
Lives have always been at stake,   dance floors   have always
been altar,   a song   isn't ever just   a song

Kanika Punwani

SISTER

My mother called me about five years back, one month into my master's program in New Jersey, right before I was about to head into class. "Listen," she said. "I need to tell you something, but I don't want you to worry."

I immediately began to worry.

"Is it Dad?" I asked.

"No, no. Dad's fine. It's your sister."

A couple of nights back, my mother had woken to my sister yelling. She ran to my sister's bed to find her seizing. When my sister finally came out of it, she was drained and disoriented but didn't remember anything. My parents took her to the hospital and had been there since. A few hours before my mother called me, the doctors informed her it was adult onset epilepsy.

"You waited *two days* to tell me?" I said.

"We didn't want to worry you until we knew everything."

"It's bad enough I'm not there. You don't have to shut me out as well."

"Oh, don't be dramatic," my mother replied.

I didn't think I was. As a newly minted MFA student, I'd been contemplating ideas of alienation and loss. I'd been writing about themes of home and belonging. I'd have conversations over post-workshop drinks with my new peers peppered with words such as "dislocation" and "code-switching." They'd respond back equally unsardonically with terms like "othering" and "cultural subordination." It was an interesting bubble to live in, but this wasn't my first time away from my family or Bombay, the city I grew up in. I'd left home to attend my final years of high school in a city 600 miles away. Two years later, I moved even farther away, leaving India to begin my undergraduate studies in Boston. While I moved back to Bombay after graduating, returning to the US five years later for my MFA had, in many ways, felt like a homecoming—that is, until my mother's phone call.

There's a dissonance to living in a separate country from your family. There are daily joys and daily tragedies that you miss, too distant and separate from you because they aren't yours to hold or behold. I checked in often with my family the week after my mother's call, but aside from that my life was undeterred. I continued writing, continued attending my grad classes, continued to go out with friends.

A few weeks later, during a call with my mother, she mentioned my sister had come down with the measles. "That's weird," I said. We'd both been vaccinated as children.

"I know," my mother agreed. "She's going through a rough patch, poor thing." The measles stayed for a month. They got worse. A thick rash grew and spread all over my sister's body.

Then, on another day, before another class, another phone call from my mother. Turns out, it wasn't the measles. The doctors had misdiagnosed. It was a reaction to the epilepsy drugs. This time they'd been in the hospital for three days before calling me. "There's a fear it might have manifested into Stevens-Johnson Syndrome," my mother told me. "Don't look that up. It sounds scarier online."

I looked it up.

I started to have this dream. In the dream, I am my mother, running toward my sister's bedroom. "Stop it, stop it, stop it," I can hear my sister scream. When I find her, she is seizing, her eyes closed. "Stop it," she mumbles. But I don't know how to.

I begin to call my sister every day. Once, she tells me that every afternoon they give her an injection that takes half an hour to administer. The needle is longer than her fingers.

"Does it hurt?" I ask.

"Yes, but usually Mom is there and she asks me questions, which helps. Today, Dad was there. He's not that good. He just sat and did his crossword and kept telling me not to think about it."

We both agree that Dad is useless.

"He texted his friend that he wouldn't be coming for bridge since his daughter was in hospital because of an adverse drug reaction," my sister tells me. "His friend messaged back: God knows what stuff kids these days are taking."

"What? That makes it sound like you're a drug addict."

"I know!"

"Did Dad at least correct him?"

"No. You know Dad. He sent back a smiley."

Twenty minutes later, when I hang up, I realise this is one of the first real conversations I've had with my sister.

This is how I find out about my sister: My mother's stomach grows strangely round when I am one and a half years old. She is thirty-six and happy that her prayers for a second child have been answered. "God is sending us a new brother or sister for you," she tells me.

I am less impressed. "Tell Him I don't want it," I say.

When people ask me what the worst thing I've ever done is, I tell them I tried to throw my sister out of our apartment window. I was two years old. My mother caught me and stopped me in time. This is a good story because it has the desired shock effect, but a happy ending: the baby hovers for a terrible moment above a 200-foot drop, but is whisked safely away in the nick of time. Intention is stopped from becoming action. It's also a safe story because it redeems me even as it inculpates me: I am two, I don't know better, I don't even remember it, though I am told it's true.

Here's what I do remember: My sister is sleeping in my old crib and I pinch her plump thigh. She wakes up crying. My sister's face actually crumples when she cries, in the way you read about in books. It's a slow process. A scrunching of the nose, a crinkling of the eyes, the cheeks collapse, the lips purse, and only then is there a wail. My mother found this whole progression so devastatingly cute that she would sometimes put a pinch of Vitamin C on my sister's tongue just to watch her face crumple, always distracting her long before the wail could emerge. I had no such inhibitions. I was always committed to see the crumple through to its predetermined end.

My sister sensed none of this. She was naturally, foolishly trusting of me. As an infant, she would automatically stop crying when I held her in my arms. By the time she was three, she was calling me "Didi," the Indian endearment for older sister. Around this time, I convinced her to let me cut her toenails with our mother's scissors. "Don't worry," I said. "I've seen Mom do it many times." The result was predictably bloody. When we fought, I always had the physical and intellectual advantage. I'd grab her hair from behind, safely away from her reach, as she clawed the air. There, that crumpling face again. Yet, ten minutes later, she'd come back, all forgotten, and we'd go back to whatever game we were playing with our dolls that day.

When I think about it now, I don't know what she saw in me, where this blind devotion came from. Now, I sometimes want to go back to that time and say, "Goddammit, kid, what the hell is wrong with you? You don't seek comfort in the same hands that dangled you off a ledge; you always keep your back up when around a person who's low enough to attack you from behind; and, if someone cuts off a chunk of your flesh, you stay away. You never, *never*, offer your foot again, one pinkie freshly bandaged, and say with a look that is both stupid and hopeful, 'Didi, maybe you need to try with a bigger nail first?'"

My sister's name is Daani, which means "the one who gives." A few years back, she got a new laptop because her old one died. It was a great laptop, much lighter and faster than mine, and I increasingly began to use it when I wanted to get some work done. This should have pissed my sister off; it would have pissed me off. Instead, she came to me one day and said I could have it. "I can use yours," she told me. "It works just fine." I felt so many things in that moment: awe, guilt, disbelief, affection. None of that is really relevant though. What *is* relevant is that I took the laptop. And, really, that's all you need to know to understand everything about my sister and me.

Flash forward to a few years after the bloodied digit. I'm no longer trying to pinch or defenestrate my sister. Instead, I am indifferent. We are not the kind of sisters who share friends or lives or secrets, even though we are in the same school. She is known by teachers in precisely the way I define her—as Kanika's younger sister. I only recently found out how much this bothered her.

She will eventually enter another kind of school. One where she can escape the label of being my sister, but also one that comes with different labels of its own: "special needs"; "alternative learning." But, before that, my sister is almost eleven. My mother was of the philosophy that, since my sister and I were born around the same time of year, we should have a combined birthday. My mother called this economy. *I* called it being cheap.

"You want cheap?" my mother would say. "I'll give you cheap. How 'bout you kids take turns celebrating in alternate years?"

Let the record note: my mother's always known how to win an argument.

That particular year though, I disenchant my mom of her notions. My sister has been held back a grade for the second time. I refuse to celebrate with nine-year-olds.

I have my birthday and it is great. For the first time, my sister and I don't have to come to a consensus on a cake design. For the first time, it is only about me, although I grudgingly agree to keep my sister on the guest list.

"How come you get to be the older sister?" my sister asks me.

"Because I came first," I say.

"So?"

"So thirteen years is bigger than eleven years. Now don't annoy me or any of my friends, okay?"

Two weeks later, when it is her turn, I am annoyed anyway. She's in some outfit she's convinced looks so good, but really doesn't match at all. It's new. She must've glanced in the mirror at least a dozen times. I roll my eyes. She wears her skirt too high.

"Hey, you know what?" she says while studying her reflection.

"What?"

"I figured it out—I'm actually older than you."

"How's that?"

"Because I'm born in 1988 and you're born in 1986. And eighty-eight is bigger than eighty-six."

"God, you're so dumb."

But even I can't put a damper on my sister's mood that day. She's filled with such idiotic excitement it irritates me, having to stay, to bear with my little sister, her little friends. I am so old at thirteen.

Here's another philosophy of my mother's—if you have a party, you have to invite everyone in your grade, her version of No Child Left Behind. Only four girls show up. They stand by the window with my sister, praying in fervent whispers for more to appear; speaking in voices overcompensatingly loud to fill up the empty space. Eight eyes alight with condemnation for those no-shows; four mouths eating seconds, thirds even, of cake meant for forty, trying to make a dent; four self-righteous martyrs praising themselves just for being there. I hate them even more than the girls who didn't make it. My sister smiles throughout. I am the one who registers the loss. I shut myself in my bedroom. I cry. I call my friends, angry, and five of them come over, bring presents, lead the younger girls away from the window and into the games my mother had planned.

This is the cementing of many firsts that will continue into long-lasting tradition. The first time that my disdain for my sister turns to protectiveness; the first time my friends will adopt her as theirs because she is mine: Kanika's younger sister, always and forever.

Kanika Punwani

The stories I'd write for my MFA workshop—those stories about alienation and loss—often featured families that were vaguely modelled around my own, with parents that invariably embodied aspects of mine, mirrored shades of the relationship I had with them—a strong mother figure, whose dynamic with the protagonist fluctuates between confidant and antagonist; a generally supportive, if mildly politically incorrect father, who acts as an anchor to the mother-daughter relationship. More often than not, a younger sister lingered in the background, butting her way into conversations with an occasional sigh or misplaced giggle that invoked slight annoyance in the protagonist, and slightly more annoyance than I'd anticipated in my workshop peers. "Do we really need the sister character?" a comment on my manuscript would read. "I don't know what the sister character adds to the story. She seems an afterthought or a device to round off the family," someone would say. I'd nod and assiduously scribble: *What is the function of the sister character?*

"Well, if you want to keep her, maybe you need more meaningful interaction between the sister and the protagonist," a girl in my workshop suggested to me. I thanked her for the well-intentioned advice, but when it came to actually executing it, found myself at a loss.

I once read that the difference between something being lost and something being *a* loss is that inherent in the word "lost" is the idea that what is lost can be found. I began to wonder though, whether the truer loss, the greatest loss, is not of something that you can't get back, but of something you never had to begin with.

I often question why my sister and I don't have the kind of relationship that so many other sisters do. Maybe it has to do with the fact that my sister was diagnosed with severe learning disabilities when she was fairly young: dyslexia, dyscalculia, the list goes on. One of the side effects of these disabilities is the effect on her emotional growth. My sister is two years younger than me. In terms of emotional maturity though, she has been evaluated as many years younger than her actual age. I tell myself this is why we don't connect in the way I've seen other sisters connect. But maybe that's just an excuse. After all, my mother doesn't have a close relationship with her younger sister either, for reasons that would take up an essay in itself, but let's just say there are no learning disabilities involved there. Can you inherit certain losses? Can they, like illnesses, be passed down from gene to defective gene?

Here's another excuse. I left home at sixteen and only really came back six years later at twenty-two. My sister and I were not around each other while we both went through a significant period of growth. While I was away, my family moved from Bombay to a small town for three years for my father's final job posting before he retired. They had a whole new life that I knew nothing about.

I used to see this as my loss. But really, it wasn't. There were no special needs schools in the town my family moved to, and my mother had to home-school my sister. My sister lost a school she loved, lost the few friends she had, lost a city in which she had spent her whole life up to that point. She and my mother fought more and more, unable to deal with the increasing amount of time they were forced to spend together every day. I went to new cities, new countries, gained new friends, new homes, new confidence. Is this how the world stays balanced? That for every gain one person makes, someone else has to lose something? Maybe this will always be the equation between my sister and me. She will continue to offer me her electronics, her dolls, her foot, her everything, and I will swallow my guilt and continue to accept. The world will maintain equilibrium. More and more, I think the reason my sister and I don't connect is because I just don't understand her. I don't understand how someone so naïve, and trusting, and *good* can survive. And I want to protect her—from the world, from herself, but most of all, from me.

After my undergrad—years before my sister was diagnosed with epilepsy, years before I enrolled in my master's program—I moved back home for a job. My mother handed off my sister to me. "You're a part of this family," she said. "She's your sister, get her to meet people closer to her age." I'd take my sister out with me, constantly feeling like her chaperone. I took her to a bar with some of my friends once, even though she doesn't drink. A friend was talking about how you can pinpoint your passions or your priorities based off your first thoughts on waking up. "What is the first thing you think about in the morning?" he asked.

Someone said work, someone said money, some people said their significant others. I said I'd often be thinking of a story. My friend looked at my sister, wanting to include her in the conversation. "What's the first thing you think about when you wake up?"

My sister sipped her Coke and looked at him like this was the most ridiculous question in the world. "Umm, breakfast?" she said.

I laughed, but my friend looked at her, stunned. He told me later that he hadn't ever met anyone in their twenties who was that simple or unaffected. It was only through my friends' eyes that I began to discover my sister's innocence, her natural, often unintentional, affection.

By the time I returned to the US five years later, my sister had started teaching kindergarten, she'd made a few friends, she was more socially confident. She seemed to have made emotional progress. I could sense my mother relaxing. I suddenly had some hope that maybe, in a few years, my sister and I would finally be able to have a meaningful relationship.

And then, the seizures.

I didn't realize how bad things were after my sister's seizure until I returned home for Christmas. My sister's face, arms, and stomach were all still marked by angry scars from the rash that were taking their time to fade. She began wearing dark, long-sleeved clothes. She rarely wanted to leave home. She lost her job because of extended medical absences. The losses weren't just hers though. They were also my mother's—my mother, who spent years teaching my sister, not just science and math, but also how to accept herself, how her disabilities didn't mean she wasn't intelligent or not worthy of love; my mother, who now watched as years of progress were erased overnight. I spent more time with my sister over that Christmas than I ever had before. I tried to take her out, talk to her.

"Encourage her passions," my mother told me. I had no idea what my sister's passions were. She played several Facebook games. I gifted her some food for her cows on Farmville, sent her a few extra lives on Candy Crush. I drew something on Draw Something. When QuizUp ranked her #1 in India in the *Orange is the New Black* category, I liked her status.

My sister's latest passion was doctors. The seizures had turned her into a hypochondriac. If she so much as sniffled, she wanted to visit an ENT doctor. She had the numbers of seven different specialists on her phone. She was afraid that anything taken with anything else would result in the same kind of allergic reaction that had caused her rash. "Can you have milk with rice?" she asked me.

"Yes," I said.

"Can I eat this even though it was cooked yesterday?"

"Yes."

"Isn't microwaving things bad?"

"No."

Sometimes lying is also a form of love.

I want this to be the kind of story where I had some kind of major breakthrough or moment of epiphany and everything changed—but life isn't as easy as those movies where a serious illness works as a device to heal all relationships. Instead, after the Christmas break I spent trying to connect with my sister during her recovery from the seizures, I went back to New Jersey and once again got lost in my own life: I was working on completing my graduate thesis; I got engaged to my long-time boyfriend, and we decided to have the wedding in India. I graduated. I moved to LA to be with my partner, and in between job hunting and engaging in marathon phone calls with my mother about my wedding outfits and guest lists and price estimates, I had little time to have any meaningful conversations with my sister.

I came back home a month before my wedding to help with the last-minute preparations. It had been two years since my sister's seizure, or what she referred to as "the incident," and she had stabilized. The medications were helping, she had a new job at a school she liked, and my mother was back on her mission to get my sister to be more independent and responsible.

Toward this end, my sister had been enlisted to help out with organizing the wedding logistics, which was no small task. What had started off as a small-scale event had mutated into a sprawling celebration spanning five days and two cities. My sister tried her level best to help, and I tried less successfully to be patient with the well intentioned disasters that sometimes were the result. I would rewrite invites riddled with spelling errors and double-check price estimates to make sure she hadn't added a zero or reversed some digits. Invariably, I'd snap—"How can you be so careless?" or "Why help if you're just going to create more work?" Invariably, my sister would hear in these comments the silent echo of older words—*God, you're so dumb!*

My sister's face still slowly crumples when she cries.

Only now, I feel guilty immediately.

I felt especially guilty because, during my wedding, my sister was indispensable. She was constantly by my side, making sure I remembered to eat, rising before me every morning so she could make sure I woke up on time. She was my shadow, picking up my handbag when I put it down to dance, handing me glasses of water before I could ask, awake and sober even when the party went on till 4 AM, so that I'd have someone to help me take off my jewellery and unzip my outfit before sleeping.

After the wedding reception dinner, when everything had concluded, after my parents and friends and cousins had all given speeches, I thanked my sister for her help.

"Did you have a good time?" I asked.

"Yes," she said. "But you never asked me to speak. Everyone else gave speeches."

"I'm sorry," I said. "Why didn't you tell me you wanted to say something?"

"I'm not supposed to tell *you*. You're supposed to ask *me*. Who doesn't ask their sister to speak at their wedding?"

It was a rare moment of assertiveness for my sister, and she was right. I made excuses to myself about how I'd done it to protect her, how I wasn't sure if it would have been too much pressure for her, if she would choke up in front of all the guests and feel embarrassed. The truth is, it hadn't occurred to me; on some horrible subconscious level, I may have even been afraid I'd be the one feeling embarrassed. I'd been grateful having my sister as my shadow, but hadn't stopped to wonder if maybe this wasn't an important occasion for her too, worthy, perhaps, of a moment in the spotlight for her as well.

"I'm sorry," I said again.

My sister smiled and shrugged it off. "It's okay."

But, of course, it wasn't. My sister's face is an open book, and when it came to the story of my wedding, I'd already recognized the unasked question flashing in her eyes.

What was the function of the sister character?

If there are indeed any moments of epiphany in this story, then my sister pushing back at not being invited to speak at my wedding is one of them, even if it's a fleeting one. For all my questioning about the relationship between my sister and me, this was the first time I'd heard her question it back, albeit in the gentlest way possible. Since then, I've noticed it happen a few more times. While I'm no longer pinching at my sister's thighs or trying to take away her gifts, I'm still not above asking her not to touch my new iPad, while simultaneously demanding to wear a dress she just bought in the same breath. Mostly, my sister still lets me get away with it, but there've been a few times of late where she'll see me eyeing a t-shirt that looks really nice on her, and she'll say, "I really like this one. You can borrow it, but you can't take it." Or I'll try and bully her into cleaning our room although the mess is mostly mine, and she'll say, "No."

And I guess it's about time she made some demands of her own.

My sister is thirty now, and even factoring in emotional maturity, she's still in the realm of finally being an adult. She's valued at a job where she teaches little children. She may still have problems with words and numbers, but she's visually creative in a way that escapes me. She's taught herself to sketch and paint and creates pieces of art that begin as a chaotic jumble of patterns and colours but seem to fit just right once she's finished, often displaying a surprising depth and maturity of theme.

Sometimes, she's a better adult than I am. I'm surprised by it every time I visit home and find myself looking to her for help instead of the other way around. She knows who to call if the toilet isn't flushing properly or if the Internet isn't working. She'll notice if our father's been coughing too frequently and bug him into making a doctor's appointment. I tell myself this is because I don't live at home anymore—the dislocations no longer hit me when I move away from family, but, rather, when I go back to visit them. I often feel like a guest trying to fit back into the rhythms of the daily life they've built without me, a life in which, in a surprising reversal, my sister has carved out a central position while I try to find my way back in. She never returns from work in a mood, but is always happy to be back home, generous in her hunger to find out what happened in my parents' lives in the few hours she was away, curious to know if there are any errands my mother needs her to run that day. "She's such a blessing to have," my mother tells me. And though I'm sure it's an innocuous comment, whenever my mother says this, I feel the undercurrents of a comparison.

And try as I might not to, I still sometimes feel that infant insecurity of the possibility that my sister might become a more integral part of my parents' lives than I am. But it also makes me wonder whether part of my sister's current growth doesn't have to do with the fact that I moved away, that she could finally grow out of my shadow and reach for the spotlight that I wouldn't willingly give her. I reach back for it at times in petty ways: insisting when I'm home that I get some time alone with my mother without my sister present, demanding that my sister and father give up the daily TV shows they like to watch together at night and invest in something I prefer watching. More often than not, my sister lets me have the win. It's so easy sometimes that I've begun to suspect it's not because she no longer knows better, but because she's indulging me; because she knows I need it, and she's always been the person who prefers to be kind rather than right. She may be the younger one, but, in many ways, my little sister is the bigger person.

Yet, despite my insecurities, if there were a way to preserve the current situation, I'd do it: keep my parents and sister fixed in the practiced harmony they've perfected—happy, healthy. I want to put a dome around them; encase them in a snow globe perched high on a shelf, safely away from any disturbances. Because I know there's likely turbulence ahead—gentle flurries of *what ifs* that could turn into a blizzard at any given moment: What if my sister falls ill again? What happens as my parents age? Or worse, what if they're no more? What if my sister is still not able to be fully independent by then? Do I move her to live in America with me? *Can* I legally do that given current immigration conditions? And, even if I manage, would I be able to provide her with as sturdy a cocoon as my parents did?

With these thoughts, everything shatters. The plastic figurines in the globe come unglued, scatter and fall. My palms grow clammy and my grip tightens around the dome; the glass spider-webs. These days, I feel, I am both the jealous sibling holding an infant over an abyss *and* the anxious mother furiously running toward her child, afraid she's not going to make it in time to save her.

Contributor Biographies

Nayomi Munaweera's debut novel, *Island of a Thousand Mirrors* (2012), won the Commonwealth Book Prize for Asia. It was longlisted for the IMPAC Dublin Literary Award and the Man Asian Literary Prize. The novel was also shortlisted for the Northern California Book Prize and the DSC Prize for South Asian Literature, and was a Target Book Club selection in January 2016. Her second novel, *What Lies Between Us*, was hailed as one of the most exciting literary releases of 2016 by venues ranging from BuzzFeed to *Elle Magazine*. She writes about the consequences of living in a female body, and her voice has been compared to that of Michael Ondaatje and Jhumpa Lahiri. The book was awarded Sri Lanka's State Literary Award for English novel. Her short fiction and nonfiction is also widely available. You can find her at www.nayomimunaweera.com

Elmaz Abinader is an author and a performer. Her most recent poetry collection, *This House, My Bones*, was the Editor's Choice for 2014 from Willow Books/Aquarius Press. Her books include a memoir, *Children of the Roojme: A Family's Journey from Lebanon*; and a book of poetry, *In the Country of My Dreams...*, which won the PEN Oakland/Josephine Miles Literary Award. Recently, she was awarded a Trailblazer Award by RAWI (Radius of Arab Writers International). Her plays include *Ramadan Moon*, *32 Mohammeds*, and *Country of Origin*. She has been a frequent contributor to Al-Jazeera English. She has been anthologized widely, including in *The New Anthology of American Poetry* and in *The Colors of Nature*. She has been a fellow at residencies in Marfa, TX (Lannan); Macedonia; Brazil; Spain; and Egypt; and a Senior Fulbright Fellow. Her teaching includes master workshops for Hedgebrook in India as well as for VORTEXT. Abinader is one of the co-founders of The Voices of Our Nations Arts Foundation (VONA/Voices), a writing workshop for writers of color. She teaches at Mills College, is a fitness instructor at the Oakland Y, and lives in Oakland with her husband, Anthony Byers. You can find her at www.elmazabinader.com.

Kay Ulanday Barrett, aka @brownroundboi, is a poet, performer, and educator, navigating life as a disabled pilipinx amerikan transgender queer in the US. Barrett has featured globally: Princeton University, UC Berkeley, Lincoln Center, Queens Museum, Chicago Historical Society, New York City Poetry Festival, Dodge Poetry Foundation, Hemispheric Institute, and National Queer Arts Festival. They are a 3x Pushcart Prize nominee and have received fellowships from Lambda Literary, VONA/Voices, Macondo, and The Home School. Their contributions are found in *Vogue*, Poets.org, *VIDA Review*, *Asian American Literary Review*, *PBS NewsHour*, *NYLON*, the *Margins*, Race Forward, *Foglifter*, *The Deaf Poets Society*, *POOR Magazine*, Fusion.net, *Trans Bodies, Trans Selves*, *Winter Tangerine*, *Apogee*, *Colorlines*, *Everyday Feminism*, *them*, the *Advocate*, and *Bitch Magazine*. They have contributions in the anthologies *Subject To Change* (Sibling Rivalry Press, 2017), *Outside the XY: Queer Black & Brown Masculinity* (Magnus Books, 2016), and *Writing the Walls Down: A Convergence of LGBTQ Voices* (Trans-Genre Press, 2015). They are a 2018 Lambda Literary Writer-In-Residence in Poetry and 2018 Guest Faculty for the Poetry Foundation & Crescendo Literary Poetry Incubator. Their first book, *When The Chant Comes*, was published by Topside Press in 2016. Their next collection, *More Than Organs*, will be published by Sibling Rivalry Press in spring 2020.

Cynthia Alessandra Briano is Director of the Rapp Saloon Reading Series at First Fridays in Santa Monica. She is also Founder of *Love*

On Demand Global, which creates custom-ordered poetry for charity. She is recipient of the Lois Morrell & John Russell Hayes Poetry Prize, a finalist in the James Hearst Poetry Prize, and has been published in the *North American Review* and *These Pages Speak*, a creative writing textbook. As a student or educator, Cynthia has been founder, co-founder, or editor of various literary arts journals, such as *Enie*, *Ourstory*, *Small Craft Warnings*, and *Treasure Chest*. She attended Swarthmore College, where she studied English literature and creative writing. She also studied global sustainability and creative writing at UCLA Extension and has received a Community Access Scholarship to the UCLA Extension Writers' Program. She is part of the founding class of the Community Literature Initiative and serves on the Board of Directors for Rhymes for Good. She has served as Literary Programs Director and Poet-in-Residence at Self-Help Graphics & Art and has taught creative writing, speech, and English literature in Thailand, the Philippines, and the Getty Villa. Cynthia is a college counselor, English literature and composition teacher, and an editorial consultant. She is a graduate student at University of California, Riverside's Palm Desert Low-Residency MFA program. You can find her at www.rappsaloon.org.

Gary Dauphin is a Haitian American writer based in Los Angeles. His nonfiction has appeared in *Artforum*, the *Village Voice*, *Vibe Magazine*, *Lacanian Ink* and the National Magazine Award–nominated *Bidoun*. He attended the Clarion West Writers Workshop in 2007 and was once described in the *New York Times* as "hard to categorize."

Originally from San Francisco, **Tongo Eisen-Martin** is a poet, movement worker, and educator. His curriculum on extrajudicial killing of Black people, *We Charge Genocide Again*, has been used as an educational and organizing tool throughout the country. His book titled *Someone's Dead Already* was nominated for a California Book Award. His latest book, *Heaven Is All Goodbyes*, was published by the City Lights Pocket Poets series, was shortlisted for the Griffin Poetry Prize, and won a California Book Award, as well as an American Book Award.

Ramy El-Etreby is a queer, Muslim, Arab American writer, performer, storyteller, and educator based in Los Angeles, California. His writings have appeared in the *Huffington Post, Queerty,* KCET, and the ground-breaking anthology *Salaam, Love: American Muslim Men on Love, Sex, and Intimacy* (Beacon Press, 2014). He is a VONA/Voices fellow and holds an MA in applied theatre from the CUNY School of Professional Studies.

A native of Gainesville, Florida, **Natalie Graham** earned her MFA in creative writing at the University of Florida and PhD in American studies at Michigan State University. Her poems have appeared in the *San Francisco Chronicle, Callaloo, New England Review,* and *Southern Humanities Review,* and her articles have appeared in the *Journal of Popular Culture* and *Transition.* She is a Cave Canem fellow and associate professor of African American studies at California State University, Fullerton. *Begin with a Failed Body,* her first full-length collection of poems, won the 2016 Cave Canem Poetry Prize. She is a co-founder of KayJo Creatives, a production company specializing in documentary film, painting, and community arts events.

Kirin Khan is a writer living in Oakland, California who calls Albuquerque, New Mexico her hometown and Peshawar, Pakistan her homeland. A 2016 VONA/Voices and 2017 Las Dos Brujas alum, 2017 PEN Emerging Voices Fellow, 2017 SF Writers Grotto Fellow, 2018 AWP Writer to Writer Mentee, and 2018–2019 Steinbeck Fellow, her writing has appeared in the *Margins, Your Impossible Voice, 7x7 LA,* and elsewhere. You can find her at www.kirinkhan.com.

Sarah LaBrie's fiction has appeared in *Guernica,* the *Literary Review, Lucky Peach,* and elsewhere. *Dreams of the new world,* an oratorio commissioned by the Los Angeles Master Chorale and developed in collaboration with 2019 Pulitzer Prize–winning composer Ellen Reid, premiered at Walt Disney Concert Hall in May 2018 and made its New York premiere at the PROTOTYPE festival in 2019. She's held residencies at Yaddo and the Virginia Center for the Creative Arts. You can find her at www.sarahlabrielivesinlosangeles.com.

Lin Y. Leong is a fantasy author. She lives in New Zealand and is currently working on her next novel. You can find her at www.linyleong.com.

Laura Lucas is a poet, fiction writer, and essayist of Polish and African-American descent. She is a VONA/Voices fellow and an Artist Trust EDGE graduate. Her writing has appeared or is forthcoming in *Bards and Sages Quarterly, Supernatural Tales, Rigorous, Poplorish, Beat the Dust, Falling Star Magazine, Line Zero, Imaginaire, Six Hens, The Poetic Pinup Revue, Vapid Kitten, Dead Housekeeping, It Starts With Hope,* and the *Unchaste Readers Anthology,* volumes 1 and 3. She lives and writes in Seattle, Washington.

L. Penelope has been writing since she could hold a pen and loves getting lost in the worlds in her head. She is an award-winning fantasy author. She lives in Maryland with her husband and their furry dependents. You can find her at www.lpenelope.com.

Alycia Pirmohamed received an MFA from the University of Oregon, and is currently a PhD student at the University of Edinburgh. She is the author of the chapbook *Faces that Fled the Wind* (BOAAT Press, forthcoming), and a 2019 recipient of both the 92Y Discovery Poetry Contest and Djanikian Scholars Program (the *Adroit Journal*). In 2018, Pirmohamed won the Ploughshares Emerging Writer's Contest in poetry.

Kanika Punwani has an MFA in creative writing from Rutgers University–Newark, where she was also a professor of English. An editor and writer, her nonfiction spans the travel, lifestyle, and culture sectors and has appeared in several Indian publications. A VONA alum, she is currently working on a debut short-story collection that deals with themes of home, identity, and migrations.

Monique Quintana is a Xicana writer and the author of the novella *Cenote City* (Clash Books, 2019). She is an associate editor at *Luna Luna Magazine,* fiction editor at *Five 2 One Magazine,* and a pop culture contributor at Clash Books. She has received fellowships from the Community of Writers at Sq. Valley, the Sundress Academy of the Arts, and has been nominated for Best of the Net. Her work has appeared in *Queen Mob's Tea House, Winter Tangerine, Grimoire, Dream Pop, Bordersenses,* and the *Acentos Review,* among other publications. You can find her at www.moniquequintana.com.

Bhaskar Caduveti Rao is a writer dividing his time between San Francisco and Mumbai. He received his master's in media arts and technology from University of California, Santa Barbara. He has attended the VONA/Voices Writing Workshop and is currently working on his first novel.

Vickie Vértiz was born and raised in Bell Gardens, a southeast Los Angeles city. Her writing is featured in the *New York Times Magazine, Spiral Orb, Huizache, Nepantla, Omniverse,* the *Los Angeles Review of Books,* KCET Departures, and the anthologies *Open the Door* (The Poetry Foundation and McSweeney's, 2013), and *The Coiled Serpent* (Tia Chucha Press, 2016), among many others. A 2018 Bread Loaf Environmental Fellow, a Macondista, and a seven-time VONA participant, Vickie was also the 2015 Lucille Clifton Scholar at the Community of Writers at Sq. Valley in Lake Tahoe. She was the 2016 Summer Resident at the University of Arizona Poetry Center. Vértiz's first full collection of poetry, *Palm Frond with Its Throat Cut,* was published in the Camino del Sol Series and won a PEN America Literary Prize in 2018. A member of Miresa, a cooperative speaker's bureau, Vickie teaches in the MFA writing program at Otis College of Art and Design.

EDITORS

Pallavi Dhawan is a writer and lawyer living in Los Angeles. She received her bachelor of arts in political science and international relations as well as her juris doctor from University of California, Los Angeles. She is an alumna of VONA/Voices, the Community of Writers at Sq. Valley, and Hedgebrook. She is working on her first novel.

Devi S. Laskar's debut novel, *The Atlas of Reds and Blues* (Counterpoint Press, 2019) has garnered praise in the *Washington Post, Chicago Review of Books, Booklist,* and elsewhere, and has appeared on most-anticipated lists in *TIME, Cosmopolitan (UK), Marie Claire, NYLON,* and the *Millions.* Laskar holds an MFA from Columbia University and an MA from the University of Illinois. A former newspaper reporter, she is now a poet, photographer, and novelist. Her work has appeared or is forthcoming from such journals as *Rattle, Tin House,* and *Crab Orchard Review.* She has been nominated for a Pushcart Prize and Best of the Net. She is an alumna of both The OpEd Project and VONA, among others. In 2017, Finishing Line Press published two of her poetry chapbooks. A native of Chapel Hill, NC, she now lives in California.

Tamika Thompson is a writer, producer, and journalist. Her fiction is forthcoming in or has been published by *Glass Mountain, Literary Orphans,* the *Matador Review, Orca,* and *Huizache,* among others. Her nonfiction is forthcoming in or has been published by the *New York Times, Los Angeles Review of Books,* the *Huffington Post, Another Chicago Magazine, MUTHA Magazine,* and PBS.org. She has attended the VONA/Voices Writing Workshop and the Community of Writers at Sq. Valley. She also has producing credits at Clear Channel Media and Entertainment, as well as at NBC and ABC News. She received a bachelor of arts in political science from Columbia University and a master of arts in journalism from the University of Southern California. She lives in the Chicago metropolitan area with her husband and two children. You can find her at www.tamikathompson.com.

Aunt Lute Books is a multicultural women's press that has been committed to publishing high-quality, culturally diverse literature since 1982. In 1990, the Aunt Lute Foundation was formed as a non-profit corporation to publish and distribute books that reflect the complex truths of women's lives and to present voices that are underrepresented in mainstream publishing. We seek work that explores the specificities of the very different histories from which we come, and the possibilities for personal and social change.

You may buy books from our website.

www.auntlute.com

aunt lute books
P.O. Box 410687
San Francisco, CA 94141
books@auntlute.com